# BLOOD MOON FEVER

## CONNAL BAIN

**Author's note:** This is a work of fiction. Names, characters, places, and incidents are the product of the author's imagination or are used fictitiously. I have taken certain liberties with the geography of both the Los Angeles and Northern Californian terrain and cityscape as they fit the needs of the story. Any resemblance to actual events, locales, or persons is coincidental.

Published by CreateSpace Indepentant Publishing

Author website: thebigadios.com

Author contact: connalbain@thebigadios.com

Cover art: midnightespresso

for Jack Ketchum, r.i.p.

# PROLOGUE:
## NORTHERN CALIFORNIA, 1870

The lodges sat at the center of a clearing surrounded by tall pines. Just to the east, an icy stream ran endlessly over a bed of small stones worn smooth by the ceaseless motion of the water. The lodges were small and well-built, the walls of logs and mud topped with overhanging roofs of thatch. Painted animal skins depicting scenes of hunts gone by hung from the entrances and swayed in the autumn breeze.

The first light of dawn filtered down through the trees, and a fine morning mist hung suspended throughout the clearing, mixing with the smoke drifting up from the embers of a large fire in the central space between the lodges. The tranquility of the morning was spiritual, as if all of the forces of nature were in a perfect balance of terrain, wildlife, and weather.

The stillness was broken only by a young girl of ten, clad in decorated buckskin and carrying a large, hollowed gourd. She emerged from beneath the flap of the southernmost lodge, blinked momentarily against the brightness of the Northern California sun, then slowly made her way to the stream and knelt on the rocks, dipping the gourd into the water and carefully watching it fill.

An explosion of crows high in the trees startled her to alertness as she nervously scanned the tree line. She saw nothing alarming and felt her pulse begin to slow to normal, the reassuring closeness of the camp enveloping her like a blanket. She rose with the dripping gourd and turned, heading back to her family's lodge, and in the process nearly bowled over the young, blue-clad Indian scout who had stealthily closed in from behind.

The scout was barely older than she, only having crossed into his teen years a few months ago. He was dressed in a rag-tag mixture of U.S. Cavalry and traditional dress, his face as frightened as her own, but he held a Spencer repeating rifle pointed squarely at her chest.

The girl stumbled backward, the gourd slipping from her hand and splashing water across her buckskin moccasins. Her mouth was drawn in a trembling bow, and she mouthed words silently in the stark terror of the visage before her. The scout stood frozen, his face a writhing contradiction of duty and pity, his finger locked in the trigger guard. For a moment all sound, the rushing stream, the wind in the tall pines, the fading calls of the crows, were drowned out by the sound of her own heartbeat and a great roaring that filled her ears from within.

She turned and fled back to the camp only to see armed soldiers emerging from the pines surrounding the clearing. They were old, haggard, their uniforms torn from the journey from the outpost far to the East. She watched with rising horror as they took up positions and aimed their weapons—so many weapons—at the entrances to the lodges. On the edge of the far side of the clearing, she saw three of them setting up a Gatling gun, which sat on its mount like a one-eyed demon with hundreds of sharp teeth strung together in a band. She turned back to the scout, whose face shifted to a pained expression of deep sorrow… and guilt. She turned back, and screamed "Watchaga! Watchaga!" until her throat felt as though it would burst as other scouts released burning arrows that flew like shooting stars into the brilliant sky, stars that fell onto thatched roofs that exploded into raging fires.

The people in the lodges swarmed out into the open, like a flurry of bees escaping a burning hive. Shouts and cries filled the morning air and mingled with the thickly swirling smoke as mothers scooped up children and men shouted to each other in the chaos. The soldiers poured fire into the crowd, and above the staccato crack of the rifles came the dreadful mechanical churning of the Gatling as it rained four hundred .45-70 shells per minute into the writhing mass of bodies caught in the triangulated fire. For several hellish moments, the camp was all screams and chaos. The girl ran crying into the smoke as around her, her people, her family, spun and tumbled to the ground, a bloody mist hanging in the air. Her mother ran to her, waving her arms in terror before being cut nearly in half by the hail of bullets. She stumbled over the nearly headless body of a boy riddled with large red holes and had a moment to stare in recognition and scream before she felt a forceful slam to her back that lifted her off her feet.

The shooting stopped. Barked commands sent soldiers and scouts moving warily into the camp. As they picked their way through the carnage, an occasional shot rang out, as the wounded were summarily executed. Several soldiers bent to one knee and vomited onto ground now stained with rivulets of fresh blood, and the scent of the pines was overpowered by the fetid stench of the abattoir.

At the center of the clearing, shrouded in smoke from the burning lodges, a man with flowing white hair in an officer's uniform stood and looked down at the body of the dead girl, his face inscrutable. He stood fixed for a moment, a frown clouding over his features, then let out a long, pained sigh. He turned, rifle notched over his shoulder, and walked away towards the trees, his boots passing over a painted skin that had become detached from one of the lodges and fallen beside the girl's body. On the skin were painted designs featuring dancing men, wolves, and something massive but only suggested that watched down over them with the enormous yellow eyes of a predator.

# BREAKOUT

# CHAPTER 1

As the car bumped across the nearly washed-out dirt road, Rachel Lewis drove with both hands clutching the steering wheel hard enough to turn her fingers white. As the rolling expanse of deeply wooded hills passed by, she cursed endlessly under her breath, risking a glance at her watch that took her eyes off the road for a life-threatening second.

"Shit!" she exploded, pressing down even harder on the accelerator, causing the Porsche to lurch even faster across the dirt.

She slowed as the car approached a bend in the road, and suddenly the woods opened to a massive clear-cut area nearly the width of a football field. She saw the squat, ugly outline of the prison in the center of the clearing, surrounded by an expanse of tree stumps and construction debris.

Pulling to the front of the administration and support building, she leapt from her car, snatching her Gucci briefcase from the passenger seat, and hustled to the front door, her high heels leaving deep divots in the dirt walk. Inside the front door, an overweight guard with a peach fuzz mustache dropped the copy of Hustler he had been perusing and stood to greet her.

"Ma'am, good afternoon. How can I…"

She cut him off, thrusting a sheaf of papers in his face and barking, "Good afternoon. I have an appointment and I'm late."

The guard examined the paperwork, eyed her momentarily, lingering a bit over her trim figure. She had worn this particular Dior business suit for just such a reason, but still couldn't help feeling a shudder of revulsion from his leer. She forced a smile to her face. The guard casually leaned across the desk and pressed the intercom button.

"Richardson here. I need someone at the front desk. There's an attorney needs escorting to the interview room."

After a few excruciating moments in the front room, the main door buzzed open and a huge guard stepped in. The muscles in his arms strained the fabric of his uniform shirt, and he had to duck as he crossed the threshold. His head was shaved, and numerous thin scars crisscrossed his skull like a spider web. *Jesus*, Rachel thought, *where do they find these gorillas?* The guard surveyed her up and down, stopping to appraise her hips and breasts, then crooked his index finger at her.

"Right," he said in a faint southern drawl, "Follow me, ma'am."

Rachel paused for a second, then followed the mountainous guard down a long corridor painted industrial green. At the end of the corridor, they paused as the guard used a key card to open a barred gate that opened into a dim, noisy, metallic hall. After opening the gate, the guard paused without looking back over his shoulder and recited in a booming baritone, "Welcome to Redwood State Penitentiary. Up here, we tell 'em, 'you survived the hood, now survive the Wood.'"

Rachel followed through the gate, purposely unfazed. From the far end of the hall came the muffled sounds of catcalls and shouts, and the shuffling sound of many soft soled shoes on concrete. They came to a stop outside a heavy metal door where a senior prison officer stood waiting impatiently. He scowled at her and took the paperwork from her hand without her offering it to him. He leisurely thumbed through the pages, then nodded curtly to the guard, who turned on his heels and returned back down the hallway. He braced Rachel with a stare, and sighed. The sickly-sweet aroma of juicy fruit assaulted her sinuses.

"Okay," he began, "Here are the rules, ma'am. He hasn't retained you as his attorney. Until he does, your conversations will be monitored. If he retains you, you will have one hour. Only at that time will any discussion become privileged. There is a button that I will point out to you. You can press it anytime to bring two officers into the room. You understand that if something happens…"

"…you have a no negotiation policy," she finished for him. "Yes, yes, you have the release I signed. I've done this before."

The officer looked at her, tight-lipped. Then he turned and unlocked the door. Rachel entered first. The room was stark, sterile, lit a bit too brightly for comfort. Two imposing metal doors faced he on the opposite side, where, no doubt, two hulking guards stood at the ready. The only furniture in the room were two metal chairs facing each other across a table. All three pieces were bolted firmly to the floor. Rachel walked briskly to one of the chairs and sat down, arranging her papers neatly in front of her. The officer shook his head in disgust and waited in the open door.

"I have to ask," he began, "Just what the hell do you hope to accomplish with this guy?" Rachel studiously read the top page in front of her, patiently ignoring him. "I mean," he continued, "you know what this is guy is, don't you? Guys like him get flushed down the can eventually, and it's his turn in the shitter. They don't end up with lawyers in fancy dress like you." Rachel continued to study the page on the desk, making occasional notes with a Mont Blanc pen. The guard reddened, "Hey, I'm..."

Suddenly, the metal doors swung open and the room was filled with the cacophony of the secure area of the prison beyond it. A rather unremarkable looking man in wrist and leg shackles stumbled into the room, helped along by a forceful shove from one of the two guards. As soon as they entered, the second guard firmly shut the doors, cutting off the shrieks and catcalls emanating from the other side. The guards guided the much smaller prisoner to the empty chair and push him into it by the shoulders. The guards secured his wrist chain through an O-ring welded to the desk, and gave it a savage yank to test it. One of the guards took a position behind the prisoner, while the other returned to the hellish sounds of what lay beyond the doors.

The prisoner sat quietly in the chair, staring firmly but non-threateningly at Rachel, who had yet to look up from her documents. The officer started to say something, then backed out of the door, slamming it shut behind him. Only then did Rachel look up from the table and lock eyes with the man sitting across from her. He was slightly smaller than average, not overly muscular, but exuding the kind of comfort with his own physicality that she rarely saw in supermax prisoners. Most of them were little more than overgrown boys who blustered and bullied their way through life. But this man looked more like an average Joe on a coffee break from work. A slightly more attractive than average Joe, she noted, but certainly not matching the rap sheet in her stack of papers. His face was lined with sun wrinkles that gave him a sense of rugged good looks, a bit like a young Robert Mitchum, but his ice-blue eyes were all Paul Newman.

"Mr. Griffon," she began, "I'm Rachel Lewis. I'm here…"

"I read your letter."

Rachel paused, flustered by the terse interruption. "Of course," she said with a slight grin, "Then you know why I'm here."

A brief silence ensued as they held their gaze.

"Well," she continued, "let's review your status then."

"I know why I'm here, too."

Rachel pursed her lips.

"I'm sure you do, Mr. Griffon," she said, dropping a hint of sarcasm. "But I think you'll find that it will serve to illustrate the magnitude of the problem I'm here to assist you with. I came a long way to meet with you here today. Humor me."

Griffon sat passively for several seconds. The guard behind him gave a loud sigh of irritation. Finally, Griffon shrugged almost imperceptibly.

"So enlighten me, counselor."

Shuffling her stack of papers, Rachel began her rehearsed monologue.

"Your early criminal history is rather unremarkable and doesn't much concern us today. I'll start with your alleged employment as a courier of narcotics and money to and from Mexico and Los Angeles. You appear to have been rather good at it. Your employers were sufficiently impressed that they entrusted you with larger and larger shipments. Eighteen months ago, you were present in Long Beach at an exchange of approximately $29.5 million in stolen diamonds for an equally valuable shipment of heroin. As the story goes, after the deal went down you killed the two couriers who received the stones. The DA presented evidence at your trial that you then proceeded to hack off the hand of the courier who had the stones in a briefcase handcuffed to his wrist."

She glanced up to see if that had any effect on Griffon, but he merely sat in his chair, his eyebrows slightly arched in polite interest.

"The next day," she continued, "an employee of a motel who also happened to be a police informant, spotted you holed up there and snitched you out. Fortunately for you, he snitched to the cops and not the cartel. The police arrived and found you there, but—surprise, surprise—no diamonds. You're a wise man in some ways, Mr. Griffon. If the Mexicans had found you instead of the cops, they would have had to keep you alive long enough to get the stones

14

back. But I do hear that their, uh, questioning tactics can be quite persuasive."

Griffon showed the faintest hint of a grin, but still said nothing.

"So, you found yourself on a double homicide rap. Not good, but you killed two men with rap sheets longer than yours, and the original owners of the stones aren't going to retrieve their merchandise by putting you in the gas chamber. There's also the possibility that you could start singing about your friends in the cartel, which, again wisely, you have not elected to do. At any rate, all of that easily constituted enough leverage to keep you off death row. But, five months into a life sentence, you go and kill another prisoner. It gets listed as self-defense, but it's still enough to earn you a transfer up here to supermax."

Lewis paused and looked firmly at Griffon. He continued to sit motionless across the table from her, as though he had all the time in the world. Which, she conceded, in a way he had. Now for the change-up.

"All that you know," she said, tapping the tip of her pen on the stack of papers. "Here's what you don't know. The Mexicans now have a contract out on you. And these aren't just any Mexicans, are they Mr. Griffon. This is Los Zetas we're talking about. Former special forces. Former security wing of the Gulf Cartel. They've been talking to other lifers up here, guys with consecutive sentences and nothing to lose. The authorities here…" she paused to glance at the guard behind him, who scowled at her, "have made no provisions to isolate you. I believe that violates your constitutional rights. If you retain me, I believe that I can get you a transfer out of here."

And there it was. Rachel felt her pulse quicken, as everything she had planned so meticulously hinged on the next few seconds. Griffon considered her, his eyes searching her face for what seemed like an eternity. Rachel steadied herself and met his gaze second for second. She pushed a paper across the table with her pen.

"It's quite simple, Mr. Griffon. Retain me and you live."

After an agonizing span of seconds, Griffon said nothing, but picked up the pen and, though encumbered by the manacles, scratched his signature across the line on the bottom of the page.

Rachel let a small smile raise her lips, then squashed it. Without looking at the guard, she said, "Mr. Griffon has just retained me as his attorney. Consequently, all further conversation is protected by attorney-client privilege pursuant to the recent clarification in *U.S. v Rodriguez*. I'll buzz you when we're done."

The guard gripped the back of Griffon's chair hard enough to bend the metal. Ugly veins popped out on the sides of his neck, and he looked as though he were about to speak but turned rapidly and exited through the metal doors.

Silence once again filled the room, and Griffon allowed a smirk to creep across his face.

"So, how much of that is true, *counselor*?" He said the word as though it were a particularly nasty strain of bacteria.

16

"Enough," Rachel smiled patronizingly. "The part that's really important is how I'm going to get you out. An associate of mine was involved in building this institution. The architects, in their infinite wisdom, decided that the correctional staff, being stuck out here in the middle of nowhere for weeks on end, would not welcome the feeling of being holed up with all of you. They might develop cabin fever, so to speak. Either that, or the corporation that owns this very much private and for-profit prison would have to pay them even more money just to get them to stay on."

"Private prison?" Griffon interjected, his right eyebrow arching.

"Yes," Rachel said smoothly. "Fully constructed and operated by a large corporation called Creative Correction Solutions. A company with their eyes very firmly locked on the profit margin. God bless American capitalism."

Griffon let out a soft chuckle.

"Anyway, they decided that the offices, dormitories, and recreational facilities for staff would all be in a non-secure section outside the perimeter of the actual prison proper. On three sides, this facility is a standard lock-up. There's fences, guard towers, the works. On the fourth side, there's a large building... the one we're in now. Running down the middle of this building is a solid wall. On the other side is a pretty average combination hotel and office block for the guards. Right now, we're still in the secure section. To get out from here, you'd have to make it through several sets of locked and guarded doors. The infirmary is in the secure section, but it adjoins the non-secure section."

"You give one hell of a pep talk," Griffon scoffed.

"How's this for pep," Lewis continued, "My associate was responsible for the construction of the infirmary. He's a very enterprising fellow, with a good eye for cutting corners and squeezing a penny until it screams. It was supposed to be tool-resistant alloy steel flat plate, but he pocketed some decent cash by mixing in aluminum plates. By now, from what he tells me, a galvanic reaction has set in and weakened the spot where those plates come together. You could punch through it with a can opener if you tried. You peel the aluminum back, and you have access to an air duct that runs between the two sections. The duct leads directly to the outside, but the exit points are all covered with heavy iron grills, and you'd need a demolition charge to deal with them. You'll have to exit through the other vent into the warden's office. Once you emerge from there, you just climb out the first window you come to."

Rachel paused, allowing for Griffon to raise a question or objection, but he remained motionless, still grinning slightly.

"Rather than waste a guard in the infirmary overnight, there's a camera mounted in a cage on the wall. And here's the thing… it doesn't work. The wiring was never done right, and the company just figured that you guys had no way of knowing that, so they didn't want to pony up the extra expense. Ever read your Jeremy Bentham? It's the panopticon meets the profit line. All you have to do is get yourself into the infirmary to break out. Once you're out, you'll still be miles from nowhere and deep in the Redwoods. They assumed that if anyone does break out, there's absolutely nowhere to go, so they can just track you down with the dogs at their leisure."

"A lot of assumptions there," Griffon noted. Rachel wasn't sure if he meant hers or the prison's, so she continued.

"There's a river that runs through the hills due west of here. On the night of the sixteenth this month, someone will be waiting for you on a raft. They'll pick you up and take you downstream where a truck will be waiting to drive you to LA. It'll be a full moon, so you'll have plenty of light and the nights still won't be too cold."

"That's very thoughtful," Griffon deadpanned, "Very generous. And all for little old me. This wouldn't have anything to do with the diamonds, would it?" He leaned forward slightly.

Rachel also leaned intimately, "Do you think I provide these services to all my clients?"

"You know the guy I killed back in Lompoc? The one that got me sent up here? He was the last person who tried to shake me down for the stones." He smiled.

Rachel returned the smile, "And now you're in here and Los Zetas already have guys lining up to kill you. Are you going to kill them all first? Put simply, Mr. Griffon, I'm your only way out."

Griffon considered. "How do I know you're not making that up?"

"You don't... not for sure anyway. But think about it. What would you do if you were them? It's only a matter of time before one of them gets to you. And even assume you survive the first attempt. Maybe then the authorities have to do something to protect you. Best case scenario is that you rot in here for the rest of your life."

"I've got another scenario for you, counselor. How about the one where I break out of here, give you the stones, and you kill me the minute you have your hands on them."

"Jake, I don't think you're that stupid. I do think that you had to have a backup plan in case the cartel got to you first. I think that you somehow hid the stones in a very public place. If you were betting on the cartel not capping you in a public place, then you seriously can't think that I will. Besides, my partner and I aren't without some sympathy for your situation. We're prepared to let you keep ten percent of the stones as a finder's fee. Call it a good will offering. That just under $3 million for you, Jake. Hey, you can trust me… I'm a lawyer."

Griffon began to chuckle despite himself, and soon the room was filled with both of their laughter.

# CHAPTER 2

Jake Griffon had fully expected to be on the receiving end of some kind of petty retribution from the guards as they escorted him back to his cell. They might not be able to stick it to the pretty, condescending attorney who ordered them out of the room like they were the wait staff, but they could certainly make him suffer for her attitude. But they had traveled no more than a few yards before the walkie-talkie on the lead guard's shoulder squawked loudly.

"Belson here," the guard said, thumbing the receiver button.

"Hold up a second," a voice said on the other end, "Warden wants Griffon in his office before you bring him back to the unit."

"Roger that," replied the guard. He looked down at Griffon and smirked. "Well, Mr. Celebrity, you're just about the most popular man we got in here today now, ain't you?"

Griffon hesitated for a moment, almost giving in to the perverse urge to be flippant, but quickly realized that with all that had just gone down, this was not the time to be pissy with the guards and risk a discipline session in one of the dark, dead-end corners of the hallway. He simply put on the thousand-yard stare and shrugged his shoulders.

"C'mon, hot shot," the guard said, steering him the other direction by the shoulder. "Move it. I ain't got all day to be your personal escort."

After buzzing through several electronic gates, they entered a hallway that would have looked at home in any generic corporate office. Griffon clicked each gate and every turn of the hall into his memory, silently counting steps so he could remember the route in complete darkness if necessary. They came to an abrupt halt outside a large, oak-paneled door. One of the guards knocked. A muffled voice from behind commanded them to enter.

The warden sat behind his desk, a mountainous slab of mahogany that dominated the room. He was in advanced middle age, but fit, looking as at home in his Brooks Brothers wool suit as a bank manager. Family pictures stood upright in the frames on the desk, which, except for a thick file, was immaculate. A uniformed officer stood at attention by his side.

The guards pushed Griffon into the room and deposited him into the chair facing the warden across the desk. He had to slightly tilt his head up to meet the warden's gaze, and smiled inwardly at the certainty that the warden's chair was elevated so that he could peer down at his underlings like a petty king on his throne. Just more bullshit amateur psychology. The guards left the room, and the remaining officer took up a position behind Griffon, carefully out of his line of sight.

The warden perched a pair of reading glasses near the end of his nose and began perusing the file, the front of which was labeled GRIFFON, JACOB E. He spent a few moments flipping through the pages, then closed the folder and looked up.

"'Hard Time' Griffon. Hmm... yes, very unexceptional. Except for that last part about the diamonds, but I frankly don't believe you pulled that one off. No, none of what's in that file makes you exceptional here, Mr. Griffon. But what does pique my interest is that you have apparently just retained a particularly unpleasant defense attorney. A Miss Rachel Lewis. Miss Lewis, it would appear, traveled all the way up here from Los Angeles today just to inform us that we were violating your civil rights."

He frowned.

"I don't like that, Jake. I don't like that at all. I don't know how we were so callously violating your civil rights. In fact, until I got word that Miss Lewis was coming here today, I didn't know your ass from a hole in the ground."

He leaned in and lowered his voice, "In double fact, we don't have a lot of trouble up here at all, and I don't like people who cause it."

Griffon had been casually scanning the office while the warden had been talking, noting both the air vent behind his desk and the particularly stunning view of the wooded hills outside the window.

"I appreciate that, sir. Nice view, by the way."

The guard slapped him on the back of his head hard enough to push him nearly out of his seat.

"Now, now, Paulson" the warden said, "No need for that. We need to be particularly careful about this man's civil rights now, don't we?" He smiled petulantly at Griffon.

23

"She told you she could get you out of here, didn't she?" he continued. "Maybe so. She's very good, this Miss Lewis. Or at least, she used to be. You might just be her ticket to restoring her reputation. She's had two arrests for cocaine possession in the past two years. She may be good enough to save her pretty little ass, but her career is going down the shitter. She's had to take any clients she can get: child molesters, meth dealers, serial rapists... and now you. She's facing disbarment within a few months, Jake. Your ticket out of here may be going to jail herself before she can do much for you."

Griffon offered only a small shrug and a friendly smile.

The warden sat back heavily in his chair. "I asked you why they called you 'Hard Time Jake' back in Lompoc. They told me about that line of yours at your trial, when they asked you why you wouldn't give up the diamonds for a reduced sentence. 'Everyone does hard time in one way or another,' wasn't that it? Well, 'Hard Time Jake,' if she does manage to get you out of here, there is one thing that I will guarantee you: you will come back, and then you really will learn the meaning of hard time."

Griffon merely turned and gazed out the window into the heavy forest no more than twenty yards from the edge of the building.

"Paulson," he said, turning to the guard, "please escort Mr. Griffon back to gen pop. And be sure that no harm comes to him along the way. After all, we need to be aware of his civil rights at all times, now, don't we?"

24

Paulson grasped Griffon by his shoulders and lifted him to his feet. As they passed through the door frame, Griffon glanced down at the officer's sidearm, the faintest ghost of a smile dawning on his features.

And at that precise moment, Rachel Lewis was walking from her car, parked as inconspicuously as possible behind a Chevron station miles from the prison. She made a direct line for the phone booth, and her gloved hand dropped a quarter in the slot. She dialed a number from memory, the phone rang once, and a man picked up.

"We're on," she said, and replaced the receiver in the cradle.

## CHAPTER 3

After breakfast the next morning, Jake Griffon felt that all-too familiar feeling of different strands of fate aligning without any effort on his part. That was the key to success in his field, he well-knew. You could plan and organize and try to force events to come together through sheer will all you want, but fate would gladly fuck everything up in a second. Too much planning created too many potentials for things to go wrong. It was so much better to simply coax the natural flow of events together and then let things develop.

He was wandering the exercise yard when things simply exploded in front of him. The sound of the huge fist connecting with the skinny Aryan Brother's face echoed in the morning air like a gunshot. The Brother, probably 175 lbs soaking wet in all his clothes, flew backward through the air and landed in a crumpled heap nearly at his feet. The owner of that fist, a behemoth of a man who ran at least 6'5" and an easy 300 lbs, turned like a cat to face the other two AB guys behind him. A flurry of swinging fists ensued, and then the bodies were joined in a writhing mass on the ground. The other prisoners in the yard, by unspoken consent, opened to give the fight room to flow, and no one seemed even slightly inclined to intervene. Griffon glided through the motionless spectators, his eyes fixed intently on the brawl. A scream pierced the encouraging shouts of the other prisoners, and something flew through the air and landed on the top of his prison-issue sneaker. A human ear. The ear slid off the toe of his sneaker, leaving a glistening trail of blood in its wake. Suddenly, he had to step out of the way as several guards raced across the yard, yelling for them to "break it up, break it up, break it the fuck up!"

The giant was quickly surrounded by guards all pointing shotguns at him, but he simply opened his hands and shrugged. He was bleeding slightly, but grinning widely and not even close to out of breath. Griffon watched as the guards led the big man away and called for medical staff to the yard on the double.

"What the hell was that?" he asked the prisoner next to him, a man whose name was either Williams or Walton.

"Some crazy asshole must have dissed Bastien, and his little AB butt buddies were stupid enough to back him. Fuckin' Frenchie loves to fight, man."

"That thing is French?" asked Griffon, cocking an eyebrow.

"Cajun," Williams-or-Walton said. "Killed a couple of college boys down South. He ran outta places down there that was worth robbing, so he took to running gash. Moved two of his top earners out to LA because he thought there be more scratch out here. The boys got screamin' on coke and messed up his bitches, beat 'em real bad an' shit, so Bastien turned 'em into gator bait with his machete. I heard they had to carry them out in little baskets."

The other prisoners began to disperse, the morning's fun temporarily over. Bastien's adversaries were being loaded onto stretchers and hauled off to the infirmary. Griffon simply stared at the carnage and then glanced in the direction that Bastien and his shotgun escorts took.  Yes, he thought, those lovely little wheels of fate were already turning.

. . .

Two days later, Griffon sat on a worn bench in the yard, feeling the warmth of the sun on his face.  Other prisoners clustered around, but paid him little attention as his attention was fixed upon a door in a large block across the yard.  Eventually, the door opened, and Bastien sauntered out into the yard like a man out for his morning stroll, the only sign of his spending two days in solitary was the slight squinting of his eyes against the bright morning sun.  Griffon roused himself and ambled over to meet him, hands at his side, palms open.  He had already rolled the sleeves of his denim shirt to the elbows to show no harm intended.

"Nice fight the other day," he said casually.

Bastien commenced not so much talking as directing a stream of consciousness at the ground, where his eyes roved constantly rather than look at Griffon.  It was like having a conversation with a caged coyote.

"T'anks, man.  Don't know what dey t'inkin', me.  Dey talkin' about hos an' shit.  I gotta take care o' dat, man.  I kill for my hos, me, dat why I here.  Dey like my employees, man... I gotta stan' up for 'em.  Jus' good bidness, man, simple as dat.  So dey start shit 'bout my employees, dat disrespect... man, I gotta take care o' dat, you know?  You know what I say?  Guards done gimme two days, man. Bastien don' care nuttin' 'bout no two days inna hole. You know worse t'ing 'bout the hole, man? No one for to talk to."

"Yeah, I can imagine," Griffon agreed. "You've been through worse on the bayou, I guess."

Bastien glanced at him sideways. "Shit, yeah, man. Dat hole bigger than my momma's shack, man. Just y'all can't go outside. No one to share wit', so it less crowded, but too quiet, ya know?"

"Yeah," said Griffon, "You were way out in the woods, huh?"

"Woods?" Bastien laughed deeply in his chest. Naw, man, I come from swamp country. All them woods underwater where I come from. We live on the mud bugs man. No one want come out dere an' mess wit us none. Shit, I shoulda stayed back there. I coulda duck back innat swamp, no one woulda found me, man. Bastien in the swamp, man? Bastien be king o' dat swamp."

Griffon put his hands to the small of his back and stretched, his head angling towards the wire and the forested hills beyond. "Think you could find your way out through these hills? I mean that's why they built this joint way out here, right? You go over the wire and there's nowhere to go."

The big man chuckled again. "Sure, man. City done fucked me up. I ain't got no experience for cities, man. Too many people. I get distracted, me. Everyt'ing move too fast. Out dere in dem woods, man, I fine. I disappear." He paused and spat on the ground. "But I stuck in here, man. Just like you. An' I ain't figured out a way over dat wire."

Griffon leaned in slightly and grinned. "That's alright, my friend... I have. I just need a man who can get me through the woods."

Bastien stood to his full height and looked down at Griffon. He seemed to consider what he had just heard. Then his face split into a wide grin. "Den Bastien is you man, man. I get you anywhere, me. Just don't wanna go myself, dat's all. I mean, man, I just don' like bein'..."

Griffon cut him off before he could work up to full-tilt conversational steam again. "So, you in?"

Bastien considered, then shrugged. "Shit, yeah, man. What de fuck else I gonna do 'round here for fun."

"Ok," said Griffon, breathing out the breath he had been holding. "one last thing, though. We're gonna need a shooter. Someone reliable, who's real good with a hand gun. Know anyone?"

"Yeah, man, come to t'ink of it, I believe I do. Hit me up at lunch. I do the introducin'."

. . .

At lunch, Griffon watched as Bastien huddled over a slender, African-American prisoner who sat at his own bench, studiously ignored by the other inmates. The two exchanged words briefly, and Griffon was struck by the incongruity of two men, looking like the road ensemble for an interracial production of *Of Mice and Men*.

Bastien motioned him over, and as they passed, he whispered, "Dat Marion Jarvis. He be your man."

Griffon slid onto the bench opposite Jarvis, who eyed him coldly. Jarvis methodically spooned beans into his mouth with a flat expression that never left his face.

"Our mutual friend over there tells me you're a veteran," Griffon opened.

"That's right."

"How'd you end up here?"

"Frame up. Same as you, right?'

Griffon smiled. "The way I hear it, it was armed robbery. That and something about a dead truck driver."

"Yeah, well, you know. Be all you can be, right?"

Griffon chuckled softly. "Y'know, I always doubted that whole pitch about learning a skill in the army. Preparing yourself for the outside world. I mean, what did they teach you?"

Between bites of beans Jarvis replied, "How to kill people."

"You good at it?"

"Rangers."

"See any action?"

"It's a possibility."

"That means you can take out a man under pretty much any conditions, right?"

Jarvis looked up at Griffon for the first time. He stopped chewing, but said nothing.

"Like a man on a raft at night," Griffon continued. "From thirty yards, maybe more."

"With what?"

"Sig Saur P226."

"Difficult."

"How difficult?"

Jarvis smiled for the first time. "Might take two rounds."

Griffon returned the smile.

"And why might you ask such a question?" asked Jarvis, pushing his tray of food away.

"Bastien and I are going over the wire. I have someone who's going to be waiting for me on a river west of here. Bastien can get us through the woods, but I need someone to cap the guy on the raft. He's only expecting me. You should be able to line him up from cover while he's focused on me."

"You got a nice way to repay a guy for doing you a favor."

"It's a business decision. No hard feelings."

"Only question left is, how are you going to get the gun? The guards inside don't carry."

"True, the inside guards don't. But the one who's the warden's errand boy does. All you and I have to do is get ourselves into the infirmary before dark on the sixteenth. We stage a fight. Bust each other up a little. Make it look worse than it is. Nothing fancy."

Jarvis nodded at Bastien. "Fine by me... but who the fuck's gonna bust him up?"

"Oh, don't worry about him," Griffon smiled. "He'll take care of himself."

. . .

Bastien sat alone on the bunk in his dark cell, stripped to his underwear, fumbling with the seam of his mattress. The hours waiting for the block to quiet, filled only with the snores of the other inmates, were excruciating. Patience did not reside alongside his other, severely limited, virtues.

He calmed himself by closing his eyes and concentrating on the smells around him; the foul stench of unflushed toilets, the stink of sweat and testosterone that hung like a miasma over the block, the ripe scent of semen drying on mattresses and human skin. Only when he was certain that he could work without raising suspicion did he begin to work his sausage-like fingers around the edge of the seam, feeling for the thin wire hidden inside the mattress ticking. Once he had carefully extracted it, he sat, glancing around him nervously, then slowly inserted the wire into the basilica vein high up on his inner forearm. He then removed the wire and raised the small wound to his mouth and began to drink. At first, it took tremendous suction to fill his mouth, but eventually, the blood flowed more freely. He suppressed his gag reflex several times, but continued to pull the blood from the wound down his throat.

When he was satisfied that he had consumed enough, he held a wadded piece of toilet paper to the wound until it began to clot. Then, with excruciating concentration, he inserted the wire almost to the tip into the great roll of fat where his inner thigh connected to his groin. He pulled on his faded denim shirt and lowered himself to his hands and knees, breathing in great gulps of air and swallowing them deeply. When he was ready, he crooked his index finger and rammed it down his throat. The blood came up in an instant, a great splash that hit the concrete floor with an audible splat. He retched again, and the remains of his dinner came out, mixed with dark, ropy strands of blood. Then he lay face down in the stinking mess and began to wait.

. . .

Abrams hated working the night shift on the block. Three more weeks, and his transfer to the minimum security club fed down in Bakersfield should come through, he reminded himself constantly. The day shift wasn't so bad, but if any batshit crazy things were going to happen in this joint, they always happened on the goddamn night shift. He had just swung around the corner of tier two, working out the number of shift hours left in three weeks, when he heard his boot land in something wet. He clicked on his maglight and looked down to see what the Christ had happened this time when he noticed the blood coming from inside the cell. He jumped back on instinct and pointed the flashlight inside as though he were aiming a pistol. In the cell, Bastien lay on the floor in a pool of filth, retching and grabbing his stomach. Bastien looked up into the halo of light, his face bathed in sweat.

"Help, man. It my gut... I ain't been right since the fight, man. Help me!"

Abrams grabbed his radio mike. "This is Abrams. I need a medic on 2C. Shit, like now!"

Bastien rolled to face the back wall, groaning miserably, but grinning as if he had just won the lottery.

. . .

The following day, both Jarvis and Griffon noted the absence of the big Cajun at breakfast. They knew enough not to signal anything to each other, but they both felt elated, wired, pumped with adrenaline. Jarvis took his tray of already-cold eggs and wrinkled gray sausages to his usual solitary bench and set it down at a slight angle, the edge overhanging the table. He began to eat bites of eggs methodically, staring into the empty space in front of him. His face was blank, but the muscles in his arms and legs were quivering slightly, as if an electric current was running steadily through them. He consciously ignored the figure of Griffon approaching from his far right, carrying a tray of food and conspicuously looking everywhere except where he was going. He began softly humming the old song under his breath, the one he hummed in the desert mountains when he waited out eternities for the targets to line up in his scope. *Cigarettes and whiskey and wild, wild women... they'll drive you crazy, they'll drive you insane...* The song his uncle used to sing to him to calm him when he had nightmares. *Cigarettes and...*

His tray crashed to the floor, spilling his breakfast over a three-foot radius. Griffon stood in front of him, his hip resting where moments before the edge of his tray balanced. He slowly set down his fork and rose to meet Griffon's stare. All conversation in the dining hall ceased, and an electric pause hung in the air. Griffon set his tray on the table and raised his hands, palms up. Jarvis smiled, then lashed out with a lightning fast right hook that missed Griffon by millimeters. Griffon grabbed Jarvis by the hair and slammed his head into the table three times, careful to allow Jarvis the chance to cushion the blows with his forearm. Hoots and screams of encouragement rang out in the hall as the other inmates smelled blood in the air, and chants of *"fight, fight, fight!"* filled the room. On the final blow, Griffon merely held firmly to the collar of Jarvis's shirt and allowed him to ram his own face down to connect with the table top. Blood squirted from Jarvis's nose and smeared across his shirt front in a crazy pattern. Jarvis swept out with his leg and cut Griffon's feet out from under him. The world turned upside down as Griffon toppled over backwards, the back of his head connecting loudly with the tile floor. Griffon lay still, his eyes rolled back in their sockets, showing only whites. Jarvis attempted to stand, but collapsed next to him.

By the time the guards got to them, the fight was over, and all that was left was the obligatory call for transport for two to the infirmary.

# CHAPTER 4

A pair of halogen headlights speared the darkness of the deep forest and rose as the black Land Rover crested the dirt trail and approached the old stone bridge spanning the unnamed tributary of the Pit River. The car came to a halt and the driver huddled over a map lit by a small pen light.

"Shit," Greg Hollister uttered contemptuously. He shone the pen light out the window, but its feeble attempt to illuminate the darkness only made it harder to see. The moon had ducked behind a large cloud, and the darkness was a living thing enfolding him. He glanced at the map again and then checked his watch. "Shit," he repeated resignedly, and he opened the driver's door. His boots landed softly in a deep pile of pine needles that shifted beneath him, and he nearly went sprawling. Steadying himself against the hood of the vehicle, he took a deep breath and nervously looked around. Nothing but the blackness of night and the sound of the river running beneath the bridge.

Christ, how he gotten himself into this? What the hell did he think he was? He knew deep down that he was more Charlie Brown than Charlie Bronson, but goddammit, that fucking Rachel Lewis could be persuasive in all the right ways. He looked down to his groin and muttered, "Well, here's another fine mess you've gotten me into, you putz." He laughed out loud at his own unintentional pun and looked to the sky. The pale light of the moon was just beginning to emerge from behind the clouds, casting a ghostly hue on the landscape. The old stones on the one-lane bridge looked like runes from a pagan site, and the thick deadfall of branches that covered the path to the river became the bones from an ancient funeral pyre. He could just pick out the narrow passage between the deadfall and the bridge foundation, a black portal that ended in the rushing of the water beneath.

With a sigh, Hollister walked to the back of the truck and opened the tailgate. He reached inside and pulled back the tarp revealing an inflatable Dropstitch two-man raft and hauled it out onto the ground. He put the small battery powered inflator into the pocket of his black windbreaker and closed the tailgate, locking the truck with his key fob. The electronic beep echoed loudly in the silence of the woods, and he looked around again. *Christ,* he thought, *there's no one for miles and I still feel like I'm being watched.* He shook off the heebie-jeebies, grabbed the raft, and headed down the path to the riverbank.

To get his mind off the reality of what he was preparing to do, he thought back to how this whole crazy mess got started, that oh-so-simple sounding conversation with Rachel that morning in his bed, the stale smell of the previous night's tequila hovering about them like a fog. His tongue tasted like burnt wood and lay thickly in his mouth, his eyes squinting against the unwelcome light of morning. My God, but she had been convincing. It was the answer to everything. It was their ticket to an island paradise in a remote land with non-existent extradition policies for people with enough cash. She spoke of long, languorous days of tropical drinks with tiny umbrellas, lounging side by side on tropical beaches, never wearing a pair of dress shoes or a tie again. And when he hesitated, her hand, so soft and yet so firm sliding up between his legs, tickling his thighs, and finally stroking him with a breathtaking slowness until he would agree to anything, anything she asked.

"Christ," he muttered, shaking off the memory, "this better be goddamn worth it." Then he remembered her hand again, the silken feeling of her lips closing over him, and he realized that, by God, it all was. He felt himself stiffen, and refocused on the matter at hand, a cool sweat breaking out on the back of his neck. Before Rachel, he had been little more than just another corrupt contractor. Cutting corners here and there, speculating on inside real estate information when he could, lying through his teeth for any attorney who would hire him for his inspection services. But Rachel... Rachel had opened his eyes to whole worlds of possibilities with her brilliant mind and talented body.

After a seemingly endless battle with the sharp branches of the deadfall, he arrived at the river's edge and set about inflating the raft. He knelt, feeling his knee sink into the mud on the bank as he unfurled the raft, and inserted the pump nozzle into the air chamber. He flicked on the pump and waited while the raft began to inflate, his mind a thousand miles away in a Caribbean paradise, almost tasting the rum that awaited him.

. . .

The darkness of the prison infirmary was nearly absolute, the only faint light other than that rising from the emergency runners along the floorboards being a dull red emergency exit sign that hung above an iron door. Two rows of beds were divided by a central aisle, five of the beds being occupied. Bastien was secured to his metal bed by a thick leather belt that ran across his stomach and ended with cuffs for his wrists. All bodies were still, except for Bastien, who was sweating in profuse concentration and exertion. He worked his fingers frantically to extract the wire from his inner thigh, nearly panicking when he thought his fingers wouldn't quite reach around the roll of fat. He felt his calm return as he finally teased the tip of the wire out, then with excruciating slowness slid it fully out and into his palm.

After ten minutes of molding the wire between his fingers and getting the proper grip, he twisted his wrist in the cuff and inserted it into the small key hole. He worked at the lock for over an hour, pausing to keep his breathing under control, forcing himself to slow down every time the frustration nearly overtook him. Just when he thought the plan was over before it could fully get up and running, he heard the clasp release and the cuff loosen. He glanced automatically to the wall-mounted camera that Griffon had sworn to him was inoperable, then, saying a silent prayer, worked his wrist free.

He moved quickly but silently to free his other hand and release the restraining belt, then quietly slid off the bed and looked around the room, his eyes well-accustomed to the gloom. Jarvis and Griffon were at opposite ends of the other row, both seemingly asleep. To his right lay two of the prisoners he himself had put in here, one with a massive head bandage that made him look like the mummy in that old black and white movie he loved so much as a child.

He smiled as he rotated his wrists, getting the blood flowing. Slowly moving between the two beds, he looked down at the prisoner to his right and raised his ham-sized fist high into the air, holding it there for a moment. Then the fist crashed straight down with enough force to dislocate the man's jaw and drive his teeth down his throat. The body jerked spasmodically, then lay still, a great crimson stain spreading across the hospital whites on the bed. The prisoner to his left sat up in fright, but Bastien locked an arm across his chest, grabbing onto his shoulder like a vise and snaked another hand under his chin. Before the man could shout, Bastien pulled both of his arms in opposite directions and a wet, ripping sound echoed in the room as the spinal cord severed and the man went limp. The smell of defecation wafted up to meet him, and he let the body collapse on the bed.

"Shit, man," he whispered to his companions, who were now rising in their beds. "Fuckin' cracker done shit his drawers." He spat on the dead man and wiped his hands on his shirt.

"It happens," said Jarvis, moving to reposition the men and cover them with the hospital blankets. "Don't lose focus."

"I hear y'all," replied Bastien, grinning despite himself. "Last thing a cracker-boy leaves…"

"No talk," cut in Griffon in a sharp whisper. "Work."

Bastien bristled for a moment, then nodded his head. The men set to work immediately. They began probing the joints between the plates on the far wall, looking for looseness, anything that would give. After a few frantic minutes, Jarvis whispered, "Here."

Griffon grabbed a stethoscope from a nearby table and tore the rubber inserts from the earpieces. He looked to where Jarvis was pointing and began working the pointed tips under the seam.. He quickly began prying the aluminum up, freeing it from the neighboring steel plate. Once he was satisfied, he stood and looked at the two men.

"You know," Jarvis whispered, "if there's no vent access behind there, we're royally fucked."

"Only one way to find out," Griffon replied. "If you're gonna be a bear, be a grizzly, right?"

He nodded to Bastien, who began wrapping his fists in surgical towels. Bastien then positioned himself in front of the wall and took in a great breath. Then he grabbed the flap of aluminum in both hands and pulled outward with all his strength. A metallic screech echoed in the room, causing both Jarvis and Griffon to jump and look at the camera's dead eye that stared menacingly at them. The plate tore free and exposed a gap nearly two feet across, and a blast of stale air filled the room. The three men stood motionless, staring into the black space between the metal plates. Then they looked from one to the other and smiled broadly.

"Ok," whispered Griffon, "You know what to do."

. . .

Paulson sat at his desk with his feet up on the blotter, dreaming luridly about Francine, his favorite dancer at Les Girls, the one with the massive Winnebagos, when the buzzer on the intercom to his left went off.

"What the fuck?" he asked, jumping in alarm. He wasn't sure if he really had fallen asleep. How could the warden, that insufferable prick, be buzzing for him this late? He had seen the warden leave for home hours ago, not having to pull a fucking double shift like he routinely did. Christ, had he snuck back in some kind of private security check-up? If he had, then this was bad. Extremely bad. Nodding off on the job was one thing, but sleeping away when the warden strolled past and entered his office would mean his job, his pension, the whole shitting works.

He hurried to his feet and straightened his uniform, his stomach roiling in anticipation, trying to come up with any excuse that might keep him his position. Checking his sidearm, he hurried down the hall to the warden's office. The door was closed. Another bad sign. No doubt he would be sitting behind his ridiculously large desk, hands folded neatly on his lap, scowling down at him over the tops of his fucking reading glasses like a goddamn school principle.

He dry-swallowed hard, then unlocked the door with his key card and opened it.

For a moment, he thought it was exactly as he feared. The warden sat in his chair, staring intently at him. But the warden didn't wear denim shirts. His eyes adjusted to the darkness enough to make out Griffon seated behind the desk, imitating the warden's disapproving scowl. Griffon's expression suddenly changed to a polite smile and he raised his hand, waggling his fingers in a perverse hello. Paulson grabbed for his sidearm, but Bastien burst from behind the open door and grabbed him in a bear hug. Jarvis moved in from the other side and delivered a punch to his chin that he saw coming, but could do nothing to prevent. Darkness flooded in over the moment of pain, and he slumped in Bastien's arms, unconscious.

"I hold him," Bastien said, "Get some'ting an' tie him up good."

Jarvis glided over to the fax machine on a side table and disconnected the cord, yanking the other end from the wall. Griffon, paying him no attention, rooted around in the desk drawer until he found what he wanted. He got up, the pearl-handled letter opener in his hand gleaming in the moonlight streaming in from the window. He calmly walked up to where Bastien held the still unconscious Paulson, and slowly slid the blade just under his ribcage and up into his heart. Paulson's body shuddered once. Jarvis looked over silently from across the room, the cable in his hands.

"Shit, man," said Bastien slowly, "Now we really do gotta go. Killin' a guard means needle city up here. Shit." He lowered Paulson's body to the ground.

Griffon calmly kneeled down and removed Paulson's handgun from its holster. He checked to make sure there was a full clip, then rose.

"Like I said," he uttered, "If you're gonna be a bear…"

"Yeah… I get it," Jarvis cut in, "Now we're all fucking grizzlies."

# CHAPTER 5

The three men jogged across a gentle incline through the redwoods. The run from the warden's window to the tree line was no more than a hundred yards, but it was the most terrifying sprint of their lives. Each man thought that if the plan was going to go wrong, this would be the killing field. They were open and exposed, the full moon casting a bright light on the grassy plain. As Griffon ran, he felt an insane itch between his shoulder blades, certain that any moment now a bright red dot would appear there followed rapidly by the slam of a slug from a high-powered rifle. The sprint lasted barely ten seconds, but time seemed to be moving in slow motion, and the dark edge of the tree line seemed impossibly far. Then it was over. They continued on without pause, darting through the thick underbrush, not daring to look back. After ten minutes of hard running, they slowed enough to pause and listen. The only sound was the wind in the trees, their branches groaning as they rubbed against each other. Griffon nodded to the two men, and they moved at a steady jog, Bastien taking the lead and pausing occasionally to check the sky and get his bearings.

At the crest of the hill, the trees opened into a wide meadow. The men stopped and caught their breath in the cooling September night. The meadow was bathed in a reddish light, the color of brick. They exchanged glances in the eerie silence.

"Christ, what the hell is that?" asked Griffon, pointing to the sky.

Above them, an enormous hunter's moon filled the sky, impossibly large and a deep red.

"Blood moon," said Bastien, still gasping for air.

"What?" asked Griffon.

"Blood moon," Bastien repeated. "Stop pointin' at it."

"What the hell is a blood moon?" Griffon asked, lowering his finger.

"It's just a lunar eclipse," said Jarvis. "It must have started when we were under that heavy tree canopy back there."

"You call it what you want, podna, but my granny a Black Water Hattie... a swamp witch. She tole me 'bout the blood moon. When dat moon turn blood red, evil walk in the red light. All dem swamp spirits come out the trees and move about. An if you point at it, you challenge the red devil hisself, and man... you don' wan' be doin' dat. He give you the blood moon fever."

"What the hell is blood moon fever?" Griffon asked exasperatedly. "No," he cut in before Bastien could answer, "Forget it. We don't have time for Cajun story hour right now. The only devils we have to worry about are the ones that could come charging up that hill from the prison after our asses. Let's move."

They crossed the meadow and climbed a steeper hill that rose briefly before falling into a gentle slope. As they descended, they found themselves on a faint but well-worn path between the boulders that studded the hill.

"So, when do I get the gun," Jarvis asked, falling in step beside Griffon as they followed Bastien's lead.

"When you need it," replied Griffon. He called ahead to Bastien, "Hey, you sure this is west?"

"I sure. I hear water movin' fast."

Griffon and Jarvis looked at each other. Jarvis shrugged his shoulders.

"There," proclaimed Bastien. "You city boys hear it now?"

They pulled to a halt and stood, listening.

"Actually, no," said Jarvis. "I don't hear a damn thing."

The two men looked at Bastien, who shook his head and chuckled. "City ears ain't much good out here. But Bastien hears all in the woods."

They prepared to move on when Jarvis put a hand on Griffon's shoulder. "There … you see it?"

Griffon squinted into the shadows, but saw nothing but rocks and timber. Jarvis placed a finger under Griffon's chin and tilted it slightly. "Look for the smoke," he whispered.

Griffon shook his head in annoyance, but then he saw it. A thin, gray line of smoke rose from behind a pine and dissipated into the sky above. He followed the smoke trail down and could faintly make out the outline of a small log cabin nestled inconspicuously in a copse of juniper trees fifty yards away. The men paused.

"What do you think," Jarvis asked.

"No lights," offered Bastien, who joined their side. "Smoke thin and pale. But we ain't crossed no tracks. If anyone home, most likely sleepin' be my guess."

"So let's see what we can find," said Griffon finally.

The men broke for cover and skirted a large outcropping of rocks, keeping to the shadows. They approached to within fifty feet of the cabin, then crawled on all fours along the trunks of the junipers until they reached the end of the cover. Griffon handed Jarvis the Sig Saur, and Jarvis slowly pulled back the slide to chamber a round, muffling the sound as best as he could with his shirt. Griffon mouthed the words, "On three," then extended his index finger, his middle, and finally his ring. The men burst from the base of the junipers and rushed the cabin. Bastien hit the door at full steam and rolled to the ground as it crashed open, splintering on its hinges and knocking the frame out of the logs. Jarvis was immediately behind him, sweeping the interior space with the gun.

The cabin was neat and Spartan, obviously unoccupied. It contained few artifacts of the modern world. The bed, if one were to call it such, was a mixture of furs and neatly folded blankets. Bone handled knives, lanterns, pots and pans, and other items of frontier survival lined the wooden shelves. Wooden carvings of fantastic creatures filled the edges of the single room, and large, ornate blankets hung from the walls. Jarvis and Griffon immediately began searching for anything that would be of practical use, but Bastien moved closer to the hanging blankets. He stood before one that depicted a bizarre hunting scene where strange, half-human creatures attacked blue-clad soldiers. His lips moved in a silent string of prayers half-remembered from childhood.

"What exactly are we looking for here? asked Jarvis.

"Could use some food," said Bastien dreamily, still captivated by the scene of carnage on the tapestry.

"We aren't going to be out here long enough to worry about food. Flashlights, fuel for the lanterns, a shotgun maybe."

"Well, I don't see any of those," said Jarvis disgustedly. "Let's get the hell out of here before some asshole deer hunter shows up."

"There's no one here," Griffon said coldly. "What the hell would they be doing out in the middle of the goddamned night, anyway? And if someone does show up, fine. If they have a jacklight and a deer rifle, all the better. It would make your job a lot easier, wouldn't it?"

"We shouldn't be wasting time here," Jarvis challenged.

"An' if no one's here, why the fire?" Bastien asked, pointing to the logs smoldering in the fireplace. "I don' like this, me. Some'ting ain't right."

Griffon sighed in exasperation. "Bastien, go outside and keep a lookout. Here, take the gun." He took the gun from Jarvis and handed it to him. "We'll be out in a minute."

Bastien looked at the gun in his hand, then shambled out the fractured door frame. Griffon and Jarvis watched as he receded into the dark of the night.

"That was a stupid move," hissed Jarvis. "Next time you try to take a gun from me, it's going to go off."

"And then how are you going to know how to signal the guy on the raft, or exactly where he will be waiting?" returned Griffon, his voice rising.

"So you give the big dummy the gun?" shot back Jarvis. "Great. Great planning *Hard Time*!" He kicked a wooden figure across the room. "Let's just get to the fucking river and get this over with. This isn't part of the plan!"

"I decide what's part of the plan!" Griffon yelled. "Now go…"

"You fools wanna wake the whole damned woods?" Bastien interrupted, standing just outside the door frame. "Jesu Christe, I could hear y'all from way over in them trees."

Griffon was about to reply when a dark shape hurtled into Bastien from the right and carried him completely out of sight. A shot rang out, followed by a horrendous shriek and a wet, ripping sound. Jarvis and Griffon ran outside and looked to the right of the yard. Bastien lay in a pool of dark blood, staring straight up at the sky. His right arm had been torn from the socket and lay several feet away, the fingers still twitching spastically. His ribs had been splintered open and stuck out from his shredded denim shirt as though they had been pulled apart. A string of ropy entrails spun out from his midsection like a lifeline, leading off into the trees, steaming and pale in the cool night air. Griffon and Jarvis knelt down, glancing in circles all around them.

"What the fuck?" whispered Jarvis.

"The gun," Griffon whispered back, "Find the goddamned gun."

"Lou… Loogarr," Bastien coughed, sending a spray of bloody mist into the air that fell back to his face in gossamer droplets. "Llll… loup garou…"

Jarvis looked at Griffon. "Lou *who?*"

Something massive crashed into them, carrying Jarvis to the ground. Griffon rolled clear, grabbing his left shoulder, which had been opened in a bloody gash. The thing dragged Jarvis away into the trees with impossible speed, and Griffon heard Jarvis's screams fade into a bubbly gurgling that set his blood to ice. The gurgling was ended abruptly by a wet, crunching sound, followed by a hideously meaty ripping. Griffon struggled to his feet and began to back away, terrified. As he moved, a dark shape emerged from the shadows where Jarvis lay, moving stealthily on all fours, then rising to an impossible height. It was still under cover of the shadows, but Griffon could make out hugely muscled shoulders and a fur-lined head that looked vaguely human, but as it turned, he saw an impossibly long jawline and two tall ears lying flat against the skull.

It sprang at him, moving with inhuman speed as a roar came from deep in its chest. Griffon raised his hands to his face, but a shot roared out, and he felt the thing fly past him, landing with a heavy thud on the grass. Griffon shot his head around to see Bastien prone on the ground, his remaining arm outstretched, holding the smoking Sig Saur and cursing incoherently in French. Griffon took a single step backward when the shape rose again and leapt into the air, landing on the Cajun. He turned and ran wildly away from the dying man's screams, now accompanied by a bone-chilling growling and the sound of tearing flesh. He ran in blind terror through the trees, leaping over rocks and logs, crashing through bushes and flailing at low-hanging branches. Behind him, he heard the thud of heavy footsteps gaining ground, accompanied by a loud snarling, and he screamed like a child. A second later, the ground gave way beneath him, and he tumbled over a cliff, cartwheeling down toward the river. He landed full in the fast moving water which carried him rapidly downstream, bouncing him off logs and rocks as it swept him around the bend.

Above him on the edge of the cliff, the outline of a hideous figure stopped and scanned the river below. It sniffed the air and uttered a frustrated growl that rose into a howl of fury and denial as it rose on its hind legs, silhouetted against the full moon that rested on the tops of the pines on the horizon.

# CHAPTER 6

The dogs moved fast, straining at their leashes as they moved through the hills. Bright spotlights stabbed at the darkness, pinwheeling crazily as the guards scrambled up the slope and began to descend a worn path. Overhead, a helicopter spun in lazy, ever-widening circles, it's massive nose light sending down a piercing white beam on the forest below. Radios squawked constantly, intermittent fragments of communication broken by the harsh rasp of static. As the dogs descended the trail, they bayed crazily, froth streaming from their mouths. They halted and sniffed first the ground, then the air. As if a silent communication passed between them, they stopped moving forward and began to circle, their howls turning into whines.

"Goddammit Warner, get those dogs going!" one of the guards yelled.

"C'mon boys," cajoled the trainer, "C'mon, get on 'em, go on!"

The dogs merely intensified their whimpering, and one of them urinated submissively. Their wrinkled bodies quivered with fear.

"Christ, Captain, I've never seen them do this. Something's not right."

"Jesus motherfucking Christ," the captain spat. "Just fucking perfect."

Four remaining guards caught up to the dogs, their leashes now hopelessly tangled. The men shouted at the dogs, but their anger only agitated them further. Suddenly, one of the guards pointed to the left and said, "There! Cabin!"

The men aimed their flashlights in unison and illuminated the cabin, the smoke emanating from the chimney now a bare trickle. The door remained splintered open, and a man sat in a woven chair on the front step. He watched the men, drinking something steaming from an old tin cup. Without comment, the guards drew their sidearms and approached steadily. The man continued to drink and watched their approach impassively. He was Native American, his graying hair pulled back in a long ponytail. He was dressed in tattered canvas pants and a burlap jacket.

"Ok!" barked the captain. "You, on the porch. Put the cup on the ground and stand with your hands behind your head!"

The man sat in silence, then took another sip from the cup.

"I'm talking to you, asshole! On your feet and hands behind your head!" The guards took up firing positions. The man hesitated a moment longer, the slowly placed the cup on the dirt and stood. He raised his arms to the sky, and for a moment looked as if he were going to offer a prayer, but bent his elbows and laced his fingers behind his neck.

A guard approached quickly, holstered his weapon, and began to pat the man down. The others entered the cabin in two-by-two formation and swept the interior with their weapons and flashlights. A voice cried out that all was clear inside. The captain turned to the man who still stood with his hands behind his head. He sighed and spit on the ground.

"We're sorry, sir. Please sit down. We had an escape at the prison and the dogs tracked their trail this way. These are very dangerous men, and... well, we couldn't take any chances."

The man lowered his hands but remained standing.

"Please," the captain repeated and motioned to the chair. The man paused, then seated himself.

"Did you see or hear anyone up here tonight. Anything at all out of the ordinary?"

"No," was the sole reply.

The captain shifted uncomfortably.

"Nothing at all?"

The man simply looked at him.

"You live up here?"

"Yes."

"How long?"

"All my life."

"But how... this cabin is on national forest territory, you know that, right?"

"The Modoc Forest is large, but the park begins twenty paces behind the cabin. Precisely twenty."

The captain opened his mouth to reply, but was cut off by one of the guards, returning from the side of the cabin.

"Sir, you need to come check this out," the guard reported excitedly.

The captain held the man's stare, then headed off with the guard at a trot. They rounded the cabin where two guards knelt by a broad expanse on the forest floor where blood, black in the moonlight, had soaked deeply into the pine needles.

The captain turned to the man at the cabin. "You know anything about this?"

"This is the forest," the man replied. "Animals hunt and are hunted. I was away hunting tonight. When I returned and saw the blood, I thought nothing of it. It is the way here in the forest."

"Sir," the guard reported, "there are signs of bodies being dragged away."

"Where?" snapped the captain.

The guard pointed behind him. "Towards the river."

"And you know nothing about this?" the captain asked the man, anger in his voice.

"It is the way of the forest."

"Right, about what I expected," the captain sneered, a thin line of red coloring his cheeks. He turned to the other guards and barked out a command. "All right, Simmons and Bailey, you two follow the trail to the river. And you," he said, pointing to the nearest guard, "bring Geronimo here back to the cabin with the rest of us. And someone shut those fucking dogs up, for Christ's sake!"

As they entered the cabin, the captain's radio mike squawked, "Sir, two bodies at the base of the cliff."

"Well," he roared into the mike, "*which* two, goddammit!"

"Looks like Jarvis and that big Cajun bastard."

"Did they fall?

"I don't know, sir. It'll take us a while to rig the ropes and get down. They're... they look all torn up."

"What the hell does that mean?"

"I'm looking at them through the glasses, and, they... they're in pieces, sir."

"*Pieces?*" the captain said, almost to himself, shooting a look at the man sitting peacefully in his chair. What the *Christ?*

"What are your orders, sir?"

The captain looked around for some semblance of sanity amidst the rapidly developing chaos around him. "Fuck," he muttered, wiping his mouth with the back of his free hand. "All right, here's what we know," he said into the mike. "We've got two bad guys down and one still in the bush. And his trail has turned to shit. That's about all we fucking know. That..." he turned to glare at the man in the chair, "and Geronimo here likely knows something he's not telling." He paused. "Rig the ropes and head down, but don't touch the bodies. And get the fucking Feds up here!"

. . .

The rain began slightly before dawn, and by mid-morning had turned into a constant flow. The man sat, having moved his chair under the cabin's narrow overhang, flanked by two guards who smoked soggy cigarettes and shuffled their feet in boredom. They raised their heads in unison as a helicopter flashed by low overhead and disappeared over the ridge. A few moments later, a man appeared on the trail, moving fast in the rain. He wore jeans and hiker's boots that were already splattered with mud to the tops of the laces. The blue-black windbreaker and cap immediately identified him as FBI. The guards scowled and crushed their butts into the mud under their boots.

The agent slowed to a walk and headed for the cabin, rainwater dripping from the bill of his cap. He shrugged his shoulders to shake the water from his jacket, looking supremely uncomfortable. He stopped to speak briefly with the captain, who pointed to the man on the porch several times, then he approached the cabin's entrance.

"Good morning, Mr. ...?"

"Chiha," the man replied.

"Mr. Chiha. I'm Agent Goodwin. I'm sorry I didn't get here sooner, but the Bureau felt it would be better for a Native American agent to talk to you." Goodwin looked at the ground and rubbed the back of his neck with his hand. "I'm afraid it took them a while to find me."

Chiha said nothing, but looked on with an amused interest.

"May we go inside for our talk?"

Chiha studied the agent with keen interest, then rose and gestured with a sweep of his arm for the agent to enter. Goodwin walked through the destroyed door and seated himself uncomfortably on a tree stump that had been fashioned to serve either as a stool or a table. He scanned the cabin gloomily and removed his hat, running his hand through his wet hair. Chiha sat stiffly on the edge of the bed, little more than a camp cot padded with thick blankets, his hands on his thighs.

"Mr. Chiha," Goodwin began, "if you don't mind my asking, what nation are you?"

"My people are called the Amaguk."

"That's not familiar to me," Goodwin sighed. "I'm not surprised, though," he muttered, almost to himself. "I only asked because my superiors think my ethnicity makes me better able to question you. They have no appreciation that I'm no more related to you than a Sicilian is to a Swede just because they're both Europeans. I'm not even... My father was Seminole, but I grew up in Los Angeles. So what we have here is two people, neither of us wanting to be here doing this, who are supposed to work a miracle in the Bureau's eyes."

Chiha considered him, seemingly lost in thought.

"Listen, Mr. Chiha," Goodwin continued, meeting the man's gaze, "I know you want all of us out of your hair, and that's going to happen. I promise. I just need a little help understanding what happened here. The more help you can be, the faster we can leave you in peace."

Chiha nodded towards the door. "Your friends do not seem to have the same opinion."

"Yeah, well... they're dog tired and mad as hell about the breakout. One of the guards was killed during the escape. To them, that's like killing family. You could say that their blood is up."

Chiha said nothing, but cocked his head. "Very well," he said, opening his palms.

"If you don't mind," Goodwin said, removing a worn leather notepad from his jacket and uncapping a pen, "You said you're from the Amaguk...nation? Tribe?"

"We are simply known as Amaguk."

"Is there a village near here? This is very close to National Park land."

"No. I am the only one."

"Beg your pardon?" Goodwin asked, looking up.

"I am the last of my kind."

Goodwin considered, his face displaying a slight skeptical frown. "Well," he said, looking around, "you certainly seem to survive well up here." He paused. "Look Mr. Chiha, this is the lowdown: three men escaped from the prison last night. They killed two prisoners and a guard on their way out. The guard had a family. We found two of the escapees dead, down the cliff at the edge of the clearing outside your door, and we're not sure yet how they died. They were in the water at the river's edge long enough for there not to be much forensic evidence we can find out here, so we'll have to wait for the lab results. We're not as worried about them as we are the third man. We haven't found a body, so we have to assume that he's still out there."

Chiha stood quickly, his body stiffening. "You don't know where this man is?"

61

"No," Goodwin said slowly. "We think he may be headed for Los Angeles. Before he went to prison, he stole something, something very valuable. It was never recovered. We think he's going to try and get it. If he does, he'll be able to go anywhere in the world. And if that happens... we'll never find him."

Chiha fixed Goodwin with a penetrating stare. "Then I must go to Los Angeles with you."

Goodwin sat back. "No, that's not necessary, Mr. Chiha. I just need to tell me everything you know... or think you know about what happened last night. Look, I don't think you helped those men in any way, but I do think you might have an idea of what happened to the two we found at the bottom of the cliff. If you saw or heard anything, it might help us catch this man. He is very dangerous. He's already killed many men."

"He is more dangerous than you think. That is why I must go with you."

"That's not possible," Goodwin said coolly but firmly.

Chiha said nothing in response, but Goodwin noted how agitated he had become. He waited for a response, but Chiha simply stood, seemingly far away in thought and worry.

"Look, if you think of anything, contact the prison... I assume you don't have a phone here. The men there will tell you how to reach me. They have my number." He reached into his shirt pocket and produced a card. "In fact, take this anyway."

Chiha took the card, and to Goodwin's amazement, sniffed it gently, then placed it on the bed.

"The men will be gone in a few hours, after they've finished with the crime scene." Goodwin stood and zipped his jacket, placing the damp FBI cap back on his head. He looked again at Chiha and said, "Anything, anything at all would be a help Mr. Chiha." He extended his hand. Chiha slowly raised his and took it, his grip amazingly firm and rough. It was like gripping sandpaper wrapped around hardwood. Goodwin turned and paused in the doorway, almost looking back, then stepped out into the rain. Chiha walked slowly to the door and watched him walk down the path and head for the cliff's edge. He raised his gaze to the sky, bruised with purple from the rain clouds, and silently began to pray.

# THE FEVER

# CHAPTER 1

The battered Ford pickup ground to a halt at the curb, belching blue smoke from its exhaust pipe, before sputtering to a long death rattle. Rachel Lewis scanned both sides of the street, which was deserted in the early morning haze. She exited the truck, pulling the Dodgers cap down firmly over her eyes, checked the street again, then set off at a brisk pace around the corner. Even though she left her car at home, driving Hollister's work truck instead, she still felt exposed.

Specterville, as this section of Long Beach was called by the older locals, was like an unflushed toilet in the midst of an otherwise increasingly upscale community. Nestled between the Coast Highway and the beach, it was once home to ceaseless warfare between the East Side Longos and the Rollin' 80s Crips as they battled over drug distribution in the beach communities. Now, with the irresistible force of gentrification eating away at the borders, Specterville had shrunk to a few squalid streets lined with dilapidated stucco houses and cinder block apartment complexes. And now even these were slowly falling to the developer's weapon of choice: renovation and overpricing. Lewis picked up her pace at the sound of either a car backfiring or a small caliber handgun rang out sharply from the next street.

She spotted the black Land Rover, caked with mud nearly up to the windows, parked in the weed-choked drive of a squat, ugly house in the process of being renovated into a faux-pueblo style

65

home. *Jesus*, she thought, *the rich finally were able to do what the cops never could—move the gangs out of the neighborhood by pricing them out.* She shook her head and let herself into the yard through the side gate. Moving to the back, she let herself into the house with a newly-minted key and locked the door behind her. Ducking under hanging sheets of construction plastic, she picked her way through the plaster debris on the hallway floor and stopped at a door—the only remaining door in the home, that was closed. She opened the series of locks, and swung the door open.

The room was bare, the floor stripped down to the foundation. She closed the door behind her, the heavy sheet metal plating reflecting the light from the bare hanging bulb in the center of the room. The room's only window was closed and covered by new steel anti-burglary bars. And in the far corner of the room, Jake Griffon lay handcuffed to an iron bed frame, his ankles similarly manacled. He appeared to be unconscious, breathing shallowly. Greg Hollister knelt by his side, adjusting an IV bottle in a stand by the bed. He rose and rushed to her.

"Jesus!" he said, grabbing her in a hug, "what took you so long?"

"You said he'd come around," she responded curtly, nodding to Griffon.

"He's getting there."

"He should be," she said, freeing herself from his embrace. "He's been in and out for more than two fucking weeks. I'm sick of paying for antibiotics, protein drinks, and every other damn thing to keep him going."

"Yeah," Hollister sulked, "well, you haven't had to feed and wash him. How do you think I feel?"

Lewis looked at him sourly, then walked over to Griffon and squatted down next to him. She slapped him once on the face.

"Hey... remember me?"

She slapped him again, harder.

Without opening his eyes, Griffon said, "Yeah, you're the crooked bitch who broke me out. What can I do for you?"

Lewis moved to slap him again, then stopped herself. "Ok, asshole, let's talk, shall we?"

"Sure... I'm not going anywhere."

"You got that right," she said, rising to her full height. "I turn on the news and find not only have you broken out of Redwood with two other guys who were not part of the plan, but that they also turned up dead and no one's saying how they died. And then there's the matter of the murdered guard. Now, if you would be so kind, why don't you tell me why I shouldn't take you out in the desert someplace and put you in a fucking hole with a fucking bullet in your head?"

Griffon cleared his throat loudly, then turned his head and spit on the floor, inches from Lewis's sneakers. "Because you need those stones, counselor. You need to get out of the country as bad as I do. The possession arrest, the impending disbarment, not to mention your role in my... my early release from prison, if you choose to call it that."

"Who told you that?" she snapped.

"The warden. Turns out he's a big fan of yours, counselor."

"Fine," she said, "None of that matters. Let's go get the diamonds and we can all be on our merry way."

Griffon raised his head feebly and nodded towards his emaciated body. "I'm not going anywhere like this, counselor. I need time. Don't worry about the stones. I put them in a very safe place. No one but me will ever find them."

"Yeah, well time is money."

"Then think of it as an investment. One with one hell of a payoff." He coughed and spat a pink glob of phlegm on the ground.

Lewis glared down at him. "Fine." She considered him briefly. "What the hell happened to you, anyway? You killed your two buddies and they took a piece out of you? The first few days you were here, you'd just babble about some wild animal every time you came to."

She reached down to pull the blanket off his shoulder, then stood straight up with a start. She turned to Hollister. "When the hell did that heal?"

"All of a sudden a few days ago," Hollister said.

The ragged gash on Griffon's shoulder and chest had healed over into pink scars that were already beginning to fade. 'Gash" was putting it lightly, a chunk of flesh the size of a porterhouse had been torn out of him. She put on hand on Griffon's forehead. The skin was cool, but she could feel the blood surging through his capillaries.

"What the hell have you been giving him," she asked Hollister, "Speed?"

"No, nothing like that," he said defensively. "Just the antibiotics and some oxy for the pain."

She turned back to Griffon. "You have two days, then we just kill you and cut our losses. Yeah, I have problems, but I'm not risking a capital murder charge on your account."

She turned and stormed out of the room, the door clanging open as she passed into the hallway. Hollister followed on her heels. They came to a newly remodeled kitchen with an empty granite island in the center. A new Viking cooktop sat in a box in the corner. A police scanner sat on the counter, squawking intermittently in the otherwise silent room.

Lewis turned and glared at Hollister. "What the hell happened to him, anyway?"

"He says he doesn't remember," Hollister replied, putting his hands in the pockets of his chinos. "It must have happened when he killed the other two he escaped with." He stared at the floor for a moment. "It was the goddamnedest thing. I was just about to get in the raft and row to the rendezvous point when he came crashing into me in the river. He damned near drowned me."

Lewis bit the nail of her ring finger.

"Look," he continued, "why don't we just kill him and get rid of the body. No one was supposed to get killed... that was the whole point. Now we're accomplices to what, five murders?"

"No," Lewis said finally. "We wait out the two days. Keep a real close eye on him. Make sure he's locked down tight. He's healing up fast... too damn fast. It's fucking spooky." She paused, lost in thought. "How are we doing for antibiotics?"

"We're good for a couple of days."

"Good. Call me if he's ready to go before the two days are up. Or if there's anything else I need to know."

"Where are you going?" Hollister whined.

"Back to work. Look, everything has to appear normal, right?"

"Yeah, but I can't stay here much longer. The gag keeps him quiet at night, but I can't keep coming up with excuses for Cindy. I'm never gone this much. I can't keep this up, Rachel!"

Lewis placed her hand on his chin and pulled him close for a long kiss. "Just two more days, babe. I promise. Then everything is ours. Remember, we're in this together. To the end." She kissed him again, sliding her tongue in his mouth. She broke the kiss, and held his hands in hers, then released him and backed away, blowing him a kiss. Hollister watched her go, feeling as though an electric current had just passed through him. His cell phone rang, and he answered it absently, then snapped to full attention.

"Hi, honey! No... no, I'm still at the builder's conference..."

## CHAPTER 2

David Goodwin sat at his desk at the Federal Building on Wilshire. Two computer monitors cast a ghostly glow on his face as he switched from one keyboard to the other, cross referencing the construction history of Redwood Penitentiary with records from the Bureau of Indian Affairs. He drew a hand across the stubble on his chin and blinked the sleep out of his eyes. A notepad filled with scribbled jottings lay on his lap.

A knock on his door broke his concentration and he responded without looking up from the computers.

"Barnett, sir," a tall man in a dark blue suit said from the doorway. "I have the info you requested.

Goodwin sighed and rubbed his eyes. Ok, he said, motioning to an empty chair. "Spill it."

Well, basically, I don't have dick. The first and only settlement I could find record of in the area was a small band of the Knights of the White Camellia who holed up there in the late 1860's." He consulted a narrow file in his lap. "They were fleeing Reconstruction in the South and wanted to set up a white's only community someplace where they wouldn't be bothered. Usual story. After that, there's nothing until they built that prison."

"What happened to them?"

"Well, no one seems to know. Seems like they traded with the nearest settlements—which were a hell of a long ways off—then they stopped coming down out of the hills and everyone just forgot about them. It could have been trouble with the Modocs or some other tribe, or an epidemic could have wiped them out." He shrugged.

"Or the army could have gone in after them," Goodwin said, checking his notes.

"Why the hell would they do that? What would the army want with a bunch of clansmen out in the ass end of nowhere?"

"I don't know," Goodwin replied. But I found a record of Grant ordering an expedition up there in 1870. There's no record of its mission, but I found an expense voucher sent to Congress. Judging from what they packed in, they were expecting trouble. They left Camp Lincoln with enough supplies and firepower to wage a small war. How many settlers are we talking about?"

Barnett looked at his file. "About fifty-eight, including women and children."

"Then I would say that an expedition of two hundred soldiers and scouts would be a bit excessive, wouldn't you?"

"Sounds like it. What was its purpose?"

Goodwin read directly from his notes, "All records destroyed in sub-basement fire, 1871." He cocked an eyebrow at Barnett.

"Ok, it's weird. But what does this have to do with finding Griffon?"

"Probably nothing," Goodwin sighed. "What about the other stuff?"

"Speaking of weirdness," Barnett began, "I checked everything with the BIA and a half dozen university professors, and no one had ever heard of this 'Amaguk' group."

"A family name, maybe?"

"I guess. But there is a word Amaguk. Means wolf. It's an Inupiat word."

"Ok, so then he's Inupiat."

"Well, maybe," Barnett said skeptically. "But the Inupiat are from Alaska, way the hell up by the Arctic Circle. He'd be a long way from home."

"So another dead end," Goodwin sighed, sitting back in his chair.

"Probably. And as far as the guy goes, no record. I mean nothing. We had him fingerprinted, voluntarily, of course, and no record anywhere. No birth certificate, no social security number. This guy has taken 'off the grid' to the extreme."

"Nothing at *all*?"

"Well, he is Indian... I mean Native American," Barnett corrected with embarrassment. "I mean, that's obvious. I did find the word Chiha in a Native mythology database. Short for Chihalenchi. Some sort of giant cannibal demon thing Northern California tribes believed in."

Goodwin laughed. "So, there it is. He's really a monster that killed the other two and then ate Griffon whole."

"Yeah, well good luck running that up the chain of command," Barnett chuckled. "So, where are you on all of this?"

"Almost three weeks out and a very cold case. Known associates: zip, chatter from Los Zetas: zip. If he's alive, he's gone way to ground."

Goodwin rubbed his eyes again and flipped a page in his notebook.

"About my last damned shot is that Griffon retained a new attorney shortly before busting out. She's already been interviewed by LAPD and the Marshals, and they got nothing. She's about the only one I haven't talked to yet, so she's up next."

"Well, Godspeed, Goodwin," Barnett joked as he stood.

"Yeah, yeah… thanks for nothing." He reached for the phone on his desk and began to dial. After a few seconds, he said, "Hi, Rachel Lewis, please."

. . .

Rachel Lewis's office looked as if it had been decorated in the midst of a severe windstorm. Precariously tilting stacks of paper covered every visible surface and bound manuscripts of trial transcriptions lay stacked like totems on a pagan landscape. Every usable inch of wall space was occupied by framed photographs, press clippings, and diplomas. Lewis was slumped in her chair, absently biting a lacquered fingernail. When the knock came at the door, she jolted upright and nearly screamed. Composing herself and taking a long, slow five-count, she stood and smoothed out her clothes. She forced a smile onto her face and walked with manufactured confidence to the door and opened it.

The man on the other side of the door was tall and ruggedly good-looking, looking more like a professional hiking guide than an FBI agent. His most-certainly prematurely graying hair was close-cropped, and lent his face an ironically boyish look. He held out his hand.

"Ms. Lewis? I'm Agent Goodwin, FBI special investigator."

Lewis shook his hand firmly and motioned to her office, "Yes, please. Come in."

Goodwin passed by her and paused, looking in vain for a place to sit.

"I'm sorry, Agent Goodwin," Lewis said, moving to lift a stack of file folders off a chair and placing them on the floor. She deliberately turned her back to him and bent to place them on the floor, hoping that the agent watched the way her pencil skirt hugged her bottom. She rose and turned to him, disappointed that he was busy studying the press clippings on the walls.

"Please," she said, "have a seat."

Goodwin sat and crossed his legs. "Thank you for seeing me on such short notice."

"You're very welcome. So, how can I be of assistance?"

Goodwin cleared his throat and began, "You were recently retained by Jake Griffon, a prisoner at Redwood Penitentiary. You had expressed a desire to get him transferred to another facility where he could be isolated under special protection because he was in danger of being murdered on the orders of Mexican narcotics traffickers. As you know, he has since taken matters into his own hands. Now Mr. Griffon is at large, most likely here in LA if he hasn't already come and gone, and we have a string of bodies left in his wake."

Lewis held his stare and smiled quizzically, "So, as I said, how can I help you?"

"I was wondering if there was anything in your conversations with Mr. Griffon that could help lead us to him."

Lewis sat back in her chair. The red light on her desk phone began to blink, but she ignored it. "Agent Goodwin, I've already gone over this with the authorities. Mr. Griffon is still my client. You know those conversations are privileged. Even if there was something, I couldn't tell you."

"Of course," Goodwin said, nonplussed. "But if he were to contact you, I would like to think that you would contact me."

"Of course," Lewis beamed, "Frankly, I don't think that's very likely. If he had trusted my ability to help, he wouldn't have gone over the wall."

Goodwin paused, measuring her with a look. "So you feel that he escaped out of fear of reprisal from the cartel."

"Why, yes. It's the only thing that makes sense. Desperate men will go to great lengths to save their skin… even the most hardened ones."

Goodwin paused again. "Maybe so," he said slowly. "In any case, here's my card."

Lewis reached across her desk and took it, offering one of hers in return. The phone light began to blink again, and this time she glanced at the incoming number. A cloud of concern washed over her face before she could hide it.

"Do you need to get that?" Goodwin asked.

"No," she stammered, composing herself. "No, it's just an unhappy former client. I'll deal with it later. Perils of the trade," she smiled. "If there's any other way I can be of assistance," she offered, "please don't hesitate to call. Now, if you'll excuse me, I have two clients with bail hearings this morning and a mountain of transcripts to wade through."

Goodwin stood. "Well, thank you for your time."

"Of course," she smiled again. Goodwin took one further glance about the office and left, closing the door behind her. She suppressed an urge to pull back the window shade to watch him leave. As she returned to her desk, the phone light blinked red again. She cursed and grabbed the receiver.

"What, goddamnit?" she yelled, "You knew I was meeting with him!"

"He's gone," Hollister's panicked voice squeaked.

"I know he's gone, you idiot! I just let him out of the office."

"No, not the cop... *he's* gone!"

Lewis rolled her eyes and opened her mouth to cut Hollister to shreds when the realization clicked in.

"Where are you?" she snapped.

"At the house."

"How long has he been gone?"

"I… I don't know. I just got here. Cindy was late for work so I had to take the kid to school."

Lewis paused, her mind spinning like a cyclone.

"Are you there?" Hollister asked breathlessly.

Lewis closed her eyes and concentrated on her breathing. "I'm here. Don't go anywhere. I'll be right over. And stop calling me on your damned cell phone. They'll never get an order to tap an attorney's office, but cells are another story."

"They're tapping our phones?" Hollister screamed.

"Get a grip, damnit! I'm just being cautious. Something you'd better fucking learn fast."

Lewis's stomach turned as she swore she could hear whimpering on his end. *How the hell did I ever get saddled with this spineless wimp for a partner?*

"Listen," she said, "Just do what I told you. I'm on my way now."

She hung up the phone before he could respond and grabbed her purse from the floor. By the time she hit the door and sprinted to her car, she was already formulating a plan, but the hanging questions loomed larger. How could Griffon have escaped from the house? It was a damned dungeon the way they had rigged it. Plus, he had enough opioids in his system to keep three men on the nod indefinitely. It couldn't happen.

She brodied away from the curb, laying rubber as she shot into the traffic lane and headed towards Lincoln Boulevard, flooring the accelerator and swinging in and out of the slower traffic. If Griffon couldn't have gotten out on his own, then what? Was Hollister so incompetent that he could leave him unchained, leave the door to the room unlocked, and forget to dose him with the meds? She couldn't believe that even he could screw up that badly? Did Griffon make a deal with him? Was he moving to cut her out? That didn't make sense either. If he was, then why the call? He'd just go with Griffon to get the diamonds and leave her holding the bag.

She cut a wide turn onto Lincoln and goosed the accelerator, flying past the slower traffic. So then, what the hell did happen? If Griffon couldn't get out on his own and if Hollister wasn't in on a double cross, then someone had to break him out. But who? Who would want... The realization hit her like a hammer to the temple. The cartel. It had to be the cartel.

She floored the accelerator, screaming past the other cars like a streak, and closed the distance to Long Beach as fast as she could. After what seemed like an eternity, she turned off Lincoln and headed down the side streets towards the safe house. As she neared her destination, more thoughts crowded in. If it was the cartel, then why weren't she and Hollister already dead? Their MO would be to kill everyone else first, then collect Griffon. Was it someone freelancing on the cartel's orders? Griffon surely had a price out on his head. She eyed young men sitting in a small pack on the hoods of old lowriders as she sped past. Could some of the local gangbangers have gotten word and put it all together? Too many damned questions.

She screeched to a stop in from of the house and ran to the front, banging her shin on a pile of lumber in the front yard.

"God *damn* it!" she yelled, grasping her leg just below the knee. She raised her palm and saw a smear of blood. "Son of a fucking *bitch* that hurt!" She hobbled to the front door, the pain throbbing down her leg. Inside, she could see Hollister on his cell, his back turned to her.

"Well, at least you're feeling better... I can't. I'm waiting for a delivery... I'll be home tonight... I don't know. Not too late."

She limped through the door and slung her purse into the corner of the room, a snub-nosed revolver in her hand at her side. Hollister's eyes opened wide.

"I gotta go, honey... the delivery's arrived. Yeah, love you too. Bye."

He killed the call and opened his mouth to speak, but Lewis bustled past him and headed towards the back room. Hollister hurried to follow.

"He was gone when I got here," he pleaded, "It's not possible."

Without looking back, Lewis answered, "What's not possible?" She entered the room with the gun raised. The room looked as though it had been tossed by a maniac. The bed sheets lay torn into bloody strips and there were deep gouges in the mattress. The chains that had restrained Griffon lay strewn across the room in

80

several pieces, and deep scratches lined the floor. The window was broken, and the security bars had been wrenched apart, twisted in all directions like a dark spider reaching out to grasp its prey. Lewis turned in astonishment to Hollister.

"What the fuck did you do, leave him a crowbar in here?"

"Christ, no! He was strapped down tight and everything was locked up when I left. Maybe someone came in a broke him out from the outside."

"I don't think so," Lewis replied, heading back through the house. Hollister trailed after her as she left the house and walked around to the back. They made their way through the narrow side path that opened to a small yard of dry, uncut grass scattered with construction debris. Lewis crouched down beneath the broken window and stared at the pile of shattered glass spread about. She picked up a piece and held it up to Hollister, the sun glinting off it like a diamond.

"All the glass is out here. The window was broken from the inside."

Hollister stared at the glass and then at the window frame. He walked to the frame, shards of glass crunching beneath his timberland boots. He stared in awe at the wooden frame and ran a finger along the line of deep grooves that had been sliced into it.

"Jesus," he said, looking down at Lewis. "What the hell happened here."

Lewis didn't answer. She stood abruptly and walked wordlessly back along the side of the house and disappeared around

81

the corner. By the time he caught up with her, she was sitting on a wooden bench in the living room. Motes of concrete dust hung suspended in the late morning sunlight filtering in through the open front door. He walked silently to a low stack of travertine tiles and sat down.

"So he's loose," Lewis began, thinking out loud. Hollister knew better than to interrupt. "Assuming the cartel doesn't get him, and believe me they're looking, we have to pray that the cops don't pick him up. That happens and we're screwed. Once he's in custody, there's nothing to stop him from rolling over on us. It's the only leverage he's got left."

"Don't you think he'll just go straight for the diamonds and head out of the country?"

Lewis shot him an acid look. "If he doesn't decide to stop by on his way out of the country and kill both of us, sure." She refocused. "I'm sure he'd like to do just that, but we've maybe got a couple days breathing space. He left here with no money, he's got no car, nothing except the clothes he's wearing. It'll take him a few days to get his shit together so he can make a grab for the stones. If he gets to them, then he can deal with us whenever he wants. If the cops pick him up first, we go to jail. If the cartel gets to him, they torture him, he tells them about us, and we die. Simple as that."

Hollister froze. "So what do we do?"

Lewis closed her eyes and raised her head to the ceiling. "We have precisely two options. One: we get him back. Two: we have him killed."

"Rachel, how do we kill him if we can't find him?"

"We're not going to. The cops will."

"Why would the cops kill him?"

Lewis lowered her head and opened her eyes, looking directly at Hollister.

"Because he's going to kill one of them."

# CHAPTER 3

Goodwin left the downtown FBI field office feeling as though he had run a marathon... several marathons, in fact. He stopped in the lobby and stretched his back, placing his hands on his hips and groaned when he heard the pops and snaps of his spine. His eyes ached from poring over countless documents, police reports, warrant applications, and the endless reams of paper that the bureau churned out like some mad Dickensian factory. He walked through the glass doors onto the upper plaza. The descending sun lit the glass building like a series of glimmering jewels, the reflection too bright to look at. He took two steps towards the sidewalk and stopped in his tracks.

He tried to speak several times, but couldn't fathom what the proper statement would be. Finally he shook his head and said in an exhausted voice, "What the hell are you doing here?"

"I told you. I must help you find this man," Chiha said. He was wearing what looked to be the same clothes as when Goodwin had interviewed him up in the woods, although they looked clean. At his feet was a small satchel that looked as if it were made out of deer hide.

Goodwin sighed. "And you couldn't just call?" he said sardonically.

Chiha did not respond.

"Ok, ok... how long have you been waiting here?"

Chiha remained silent.

"Where are you staying?"

Silence.

Goodwin stood for a moment, then dropped his head. "Come on," he said, motioning with a finger for the man to follow, walking tiredly past him.

"Where?" asked Chiha, turning but not moving his feet yet.

Goodwin stopped and turned back. "I'm going to buy you dinner," he sighed. "Come on, it's not like I have anything else productive to do."

He turned to walk to his Lexus, not hearing Chiha following him, but feeling his presence just over his left shoulder nonetheless.

The drive to the restaurant was a study in minimalist conversation. Goodwin made several attempts to engage his passenger in small talk, but received nothing but a passive silence in return. As he turned off Wilshire onto Westwood heading to Fundamental LA, his favorite eatery near the field office, he couldn't help but sneak glances at the man next to him as he drove. Chiha sat in complete stillness, as though physically present but otherwise very much far away somewhere. Goodwin sensed a calm reserve about him, but there was something else as well, something like an anxious concern that contradicted his placid demeanor. It was only after sitting down at a table and picking listlessly at his chicken salad for ten minutes that the man spoke.

"How close are you to finding him?"

Goodwin faked astonishment, "He speaks!"

Chiha simply looked at him.

Goodwin raised his hands in mock surrender. "Griffon? Not very."

"You are still sure that he is in this city?"

Goodwin pushed his plate away across the table and said, "Right now there isn't very much I'm sure of at all. For instance, I'm not sure what you're doing here. I'm not sure how you got here. In fact, I'm not altogether sure that you exist."

Chiha looked confused. "I am here."

Goodwin shook his head in resignation. "Oh, you're here alright. The only thing is, after being sent on a six hundred mile trip that ends halfway up a mountain in a rainstorm, I get to interview someone of whom there is no record. Not a trace. There isn't even supposed to be anyone living up there. There's no record of villages, settlements, or anything for over a hundred years. You have no birth certificate, no driver's license, no social security number, no deed to the land. Nothing. Please understand, the system doesn't deal well with this sort of thing."

"Maybe your system does not know everything. Maybe it is not all powerful."

Goodwin half-smiled and gazed out the window.

Chiha followed his gaze and caught the expression on his face. Out on the street, throngs of people were making their way along the sidewalk at the end of the day and traffic had snarled to a standstill.

"You live among all these people. Yet you are so alone."

Goodwin snapped his head back to the man across the table. Then he grinned mildly, "That's interesting, coming from you."

Chiha's lips curled upward, but the look was far too sad to be termed a smile.

"I am the last of my people. I live in a far place. I should be alone."

"But you have no family, no friends? Nothing?"

Chiha paused, then spoke, "They are gone. Like the rest of my people. Yet, as long as I live, they live. They are in my blood and in my heart."

Goodwin considered for a moment. "You really believe that?"

"Yes."

Goodwin raised his coffee cup to his lips and looked Chiha firmly in the eyes. "Then here's to you. My heart isn't big enough to hold the people I've lost."

"Then where is your family if not in your heart?"

Goodwin smiled, "Which one? Which family, I mean, not which heart."

Chiha looked at him blankly.

"Let's just say I've had a bad record with families." He took another sip of coffee. "I was the golden boy in our community. I had one long string of scholarships and everyone loved me until I decided to turn that into a career with the Bureau."

Chiha continued to look confused.

"It's like this," Goodwin sighed. "My father was a Seminole. Saw himself as the last great warrior. If he had his way, I would have grown up in some godforsaken swamp with the alligators and the sawgrass. But my mother was half Scott, and she insisted on living in town. You know the Seminoles, right. Only Indian group never to formally declare an end to their little series of wars with the government. My father claimed he could trace his heritage all the way down to Osceola, but that's probably booze-fueled bullshit. When I was a kid, he went up to Pine Ridge after AIM liberated Wounded Knee. Was going to join the great uprising. But he got there just in time to see the FBI hold it under siege. He thought my wanting to join the Bureau was a personal attack on him."

Goodwin paused and took another swallow of coffee. "He died in a car accident while I was still in school. I never got to explain it to him. My mother looked at me at the funeral but she couldn't bring herself to say a word."

The two men sat in silence for a while. The waitress came over to ask if Goodwin would like more coffee, but he shooed her away with his hand.

At last, Chiha spoke. "So why do this? Why join the FBI?"

Goodwin seemed to pull himself out of intense self-reflection. "Ah, now that's the other side of the story. My second family. When I went away to college I was full of bright ideas about how I was going to fulfill everyone's dreams for me. Law enforcement was about the farthest thing from my mind. I wanted to do law, because that was where the real change happened. The

Bureau has an entry level to the special agent category for lawyers, and I thought that was where my calling was. And in the midst of that… I fell in love."

Goodwin looked out the window again, as if scanning the passers-by for a specific face. Chiha continued to watch him intensely.

"She was a white woman. Her family got used to me about as much as you could expect, but I didn't tell my family about her. That's what you're supposed to do in college—go off and do all the things that your parents are afraid you might do. Our senior year, we moved in together. We were both working and we found a little studio off campus and moved in. She was coming out of a movie one night while I was at class, and three kids accosted her while she was getting into her car. One of them stuck a gun in her ribs. She screamed for help and an off duty cop heard her. She got hit in the crossfire. Her femoral artery. She bled out before the ambulance could even get there, and I don't know why I'm telling you all this."

Goodwin wiped his forehead. A film of perspiration had begun to form there, and he noticed his hand trembling. This might be the craziest of circumstances, but it felt good to finally say all of this.

"Sometimes it is good to talk," Chiha said.

Goodwin shrugged his shoulders.

"The case was a slam dunk for the DA. They got life without parole on the felony murder rule. The only reason the DA didn't go for the death penalty was that they were all seventeen years old. I went into the courtroom to see evil. To see it punished. All I saw was three kids break down and cry when the judge sentenced them. Just three kids shitting their pants when they saw what was real, what they had done, and what was in store for them. That was supposed to be closure for me."

He smiled hauntingly.

"It didn't do a damn thing, though. I wanted to see evil so I could stare it down, and all I saw was three kids hooked on heroin trying to score enough money for their fix. There was a bigger evil at play. So I joined the Bureau to look evil dead on in the face. I hooked up with Behavioral Sciences and tried profiling serial killers. I had a knack for it, turns out. So I ended up getting what I wanted and losing everything I loved in the process. I'm about as far from my father's life as I could get. And the damnedest thing is... I've seen every inhuman act one man can commit against another, brutality so monstrous it would keep most people from ever sleeping again. But instead of evil, all I saw was a twisted psychological banality. The killers I tracked weren't evil with a capital E... they were petty and mundane, like the fucking Nazi bureaucrats in the war. You'd think I'd find true evil given the hundreds of cases I've worked, but I haven't laid eyes on it yet."

Chiha stared at him, seeming lost in some very inner recess. At length, he said softy, "Perhaps soon, you will."

# CHAPTER 4

The small Craftsman home was dark, setting it apart from its similar neighbors that lined the shaded street. The house sat on the end of the street at the verge of a small canyon thick with scrub brush and Mexican sage that filled the air with a heavy scent. Two tall pepper trees rose from the small, fenced in back yard and partially shaded the back of the house, casting long shadows over the sloped roof. A few leaves shook free of the branches and spiraled down to the tile patio and then a figure hung suspended from one limb, swung briefly in the evening breeze, and dropped to the ground. He shook his head to clear it from an inner fog and crouched beside a large, built-in grill. The moon, a hair away from full, briefly emerged from a gossamer stretch of clouds, illuminating the yard in a ghostly shade of bone.

The last thing Griffon remembered clearly was lying chained down on the cot and feeling as if he were being eaten alive by fire ants. It had begun as a maddening itch on the faint scars that remained on his body, then built to an unbearable fire. The room seemed to go red, as if misted with a film of blood, and then there was darkness. When he came to, he was in an alley around the corner from the house where he had been chained like an animal, panting and slick with sweat. The muscles in his back ached, as did his fingers and jaw. Even his teeth hurt, as though he had bitten down hard on metal.

.

But even though his body felt rubbery, his survival instinct was hard and razor sharp. There was a time to sit back and figure things out, and then there was a time to run. Run time was definitely now—connecting the dots could come later.

He kept mostly to the alleys, slipping in and out of the parked cars and trash cans until he emerged into a more middle-class neighborhood with a broad park on the far side of the street. He looked at his clothes, torn and stained, and sorely missed having shoes on his feet, but figured that he looked like just another homeless man, one of the unseen amidst the masses. He risked the hurried scramble across the street to the park and took in the scene. Mercifully, it was mostly empty, but he still slunk around the outer edge until he reached a small, chain-link fence, beyond which lay a narrow arroyo that widened into a larger brush canyon. He picked his way along a barely visible path, following the old and faded tracks of the urban coyotes that marked the trail.

The trail narrowed to a point where he feared he could no longer wind his way through, then opened to face a small canyon slope, beyond which he could see the tops of a row of rooftops. Gauging the time of day by the descending sun, he found a small open space between two Hawthorne bushes and settled down to wait for night to fall. The work he had planned required darkness.

Now, hunkered down beside the grill, he put his plan into action. He moved silently to what looked like a bedroom window that was open less than five inches, not much... but hopefully enough. He peered through the glass and saw that a wooden dowel was positioned in the window track that prevented the window from opening any farther. Drawing in a breath, he slid his right arm through the opening, reaching in as far as he could get to turn his arm and try to dislodge the dowel. The metal frame bit sharply into his forearm as he strained to push enough of his arm through to reach the track, but the dowel remained one maddening inch from his straining fingers.

He gritted his teeth and strained until beads of sweat popped from his skin and the veins in his face and neck stood out like chords. The moon had fully emerged from the clouds and somewhere in the canyon behind the house. A rabbit screamed once, then the sound was drowned out by the cries of coyotes. Griffon strained again, his body vibrating like tuning fork, and a series of convulsions rocked his body. Then, almost imperceptibly, the tips of his fingers began to elongate, stretching both skin and nail, until they brushed the edge of the dowel. A rushing sound, like a broken dam, filled his ears, and the fingers grew slightly longer, the nails growing longer and more pointed. The tips of the nails of his first two fingers caught beneath the rough wood of the dowel, and with a whispered shriek, he flicked the dowel free where it clattered to the floor.

Griffon withdrew his arm and stared for a moment at his hand, the fingers now returned to normal, but throbbing with energy. "What the fuck?" he whispered, turning to look at his palm. A faint shadow of stubble, like a face after a shave with a dull razor, covered most of the skin. He shook his head slightly, then refocused on the open window. Again, there was a time to figure out just what the hell was going on later; it was time to get his ass in gear now.

He gently slid the window open and peered into the darkened room. The large bedroom was tastefully, if somewhat inexpensively, decorated. Satisfied that all was silent in the house, he hoisted himself up over the sill and slipped soundlessly into the room. Wasting no time, he headed straight for the closet. Both sides were filled top to bottom with women's clothes, and he swore under his breath. Scanning the dark room, he noticed the tall, cherry wood dresser in the far corner. He rushed to it and began pulling open drawers, feeling nervous and fidgety... uncharacteristically unprofessional. The top drawer held sock and boxer-briefs, handfuls of which he tossed on the four-poster bed behind him. The lower drawers held an array of t-shirts and blue jeans. He scooped up several and set them on top of the dresser. Stripping quickly, he grabbed a pair of underwear and found it a little loose in the waste, but workable. The same was true of the jeans. They were several inches too long, but rolling the cuffs made them look presentable, and a canvas belt he found in the underwear drawer cinched them snugly around his waist. He grabbed a plain gray t-shirt that gave him plenty of breathing room, but still didn't look too unusually large and hunted about for shoes.

He found them under the bed, and swore as soon as he held up a pair of tan loafers. They were at least two sizes too big. He was about to hurl one across the room when he spotted a worn pair of Sanuk flip flops poking out from under the bed. He slipped them on, and although far too large for him, they worked better than the shoes would have.

He scrutinized himself in the mirrored closet doors. Not too bad for dumb luck. He could almost pass himself off as a slightly over-the-hill surf bum. Perfect for blending into the background of a beach community. He rolled up the tattered remains of his old clothes was about to toss the house for any quick cash or...food? Why in the hell did he want food at a time like this? He wrinkled his brow at the conundrum, then looked up sharply and froze, listening intently.

He distinctly heard the faint crunch of tires on gravel and knew that a car had just rolled into the drive at the front of the house. He shook his head again, thinking he was crazy. He was all the way around the back in the bedroom. There was no way he could hear a car in the drive. But, nonetheless, he intuited more than heard the metallic clink of a car door, then footsteps up the path.

Acting on pure instinct, he shut down the rational part of his brain and dove headfirst through the window. He hit the patio in a tuck-and-roll and was instantly up on his feet and running for the canyon and the protective layer of brush. He vaulted the fence on the fly, one hand faintly pushing himself up to clear the top, then dropped to the sloping canyon wall, his feet picking their way down the loose terrain as if driven by a power all their own. Once at the bottom, he turned and looked at the fence top high above him, his eyes wide. He wasn't even slightly out of breath, and he felt his heart-rate slowly murmur as though he were calmly sitting in a comfortable chair reading the newspaper. He looked to the purple sky to see the moon slip half behind a shadow of cloud, and he grinned wildly, feeling a rising power coursing through his veins.

He stuffed his hands in the front pockets of his jeans and came out with two rumpled twenty dollar bills that had clearly made the full circuit through the washer and dryer. He stared at the bills. The dried edges scratched against the stubbly growth of hair on his palms, and his smile widened into a toothy jack o' lantern grin. *When the good luck comes, baby, it comes in spades*, he thought and laughed a deep, rumbling chuckle. Ahead, a rabbit, alerted by the sound, tore out from a patch of sage, kicking gravel up behind it as it zigzagged up the trail. Griffon had to suppress a sudden urge to give chase, and instead forced himself to retrace his steps through the canyon, looking for the streetlights as a guide to his exit point. The night around him was filled with a rich and heady cornucopia of sounds and scents. He felt alive, more than alive. He felt as if he owned the night.

# CHAPTER 5

The Chopping Mall, a seedy garage off an alley near East Seventh Street, was bustling. Welding spark flew out from beneath several cars, and the deafening sound of grinding metal and the pumping of pistons bled out messily into the street. Empty cases of tall boys rose like monoliths from the oil and grease stained cement floor, and the air stunk of gasoline and motor oil.

Warren—he was always only known as just Warren No Last Name—was busy at work on a dented Ford Falcon. He lowered the battered welding mask to his face and clicked on his torch, the flame reflecting off the protective shield like St. Elmo's fire.

"Warren!" a phlegmy voice echoed through the garage, "Call in the office."

Warren switched off his torch, lifted the mask, and turned his head.

"Well," the manager boomed, "you gonna wait all day or take this and get back to work?"

Warren smiled as he slipped the mask from his head and took a small pair of wire-rimmed glasses from his pocket, positioning them on his nose. Wiping his hands on his denim overalls, he set the mask down and strolled across the floor.

"Someone on the office phone for me?" he said coolly as he passed the manager.

"One of your bitches, sounds like. Don't take all damn day."

Warren paused and looked back over his shoulder at the manager, holding his stare with cool and predatory eyes. The manager shuffled his feet uncomfortably. Noting this with a grin, Warren entered the office and closed the door. He pulled an American Spirit from a battered pack and lit it with a death's head zippo, leaving the cigarette dangling from his lips. The phone lay half buried beneath a cascading pile of bills of lading and orders for parts.

"Yeah?" he said into the receiver.

"You said if I ever need a favor..." Rachel Lewis began.

"Yeah?" he repeated.

"I have a job for you."

"I also said something about money."

"How much?"

"Ten now, ten when it's over."

A pause sat on the line, then Lewis said, "Ok, but there's one more thing."

Warren exhaled smoke into the room. "There always is, isn't there," he sighed.

"I need this to be cowboy."

"That changes things."

"How much does it change things?"

"When does this cowboy need to ride?"

"As soon as he can saddle up."

"Twenty now, twenty when it's over."

"*Oh Jesus fuck*, I can't do that on short notice!"

"How do you think the cowboy feels?" A long silence stretched across the distance. "Ok, listen. I know I owe you one, so ten now, the rest after. And you can knock five off the balance. Call it a professional discount."

Lewis considered. "Fine. I'll have the details to you tonight."

"Green dumpster behind the shop. Leave everything underneath in a brown envelope between 8:30 and 8:45. I'll pick it up when I get off."

"It'll be there."

"Always a pleasure," he said and hung up. He took a long drag off his smoke and exhaled deeply, looking about the manager's office. A calendar on the wall showed two impossibly endowed young women in latex servicing a horse. He laughed. "Ain't life just fuckin' grand," he said to the room, then returned to the Falcon.

. . .

Rachel Lewis hung up the pay phone and walked back towards her Porsche. The reality of the conversation she just had slammed home to her with a force that weakened her knees, and she fought for balance on the litter-strewn street. *A cop*, she thought, *Jesus Christ, not just a cop, but a fed. Did I really just order the killing of an FBI agent?* She shook her head to clear her thoughts and clenched her fists to will the thoughts away. This was business, simple expedient business. Once she had the diamonds and was set up on a very distant tropical beach, none of it would matter. She just had to buy time and shift the focus away from her. The natural assumption would be that Griffon killed Goodwin, and he was going to be dead himself shortly after Goodwin met his grand exit. The plan would work. The plan had to work.

She set her eyes on the Porsche and walked quickly towards it, heels clacking loudly along the deserted sidewalk. As she reached for her keys, she felt a hand grasp her roughly by the shoulder and spin her around. She filled her lungs to scream, but stopped as she faced five Hispanic men, all with shaved heads, but dressed in matching black business suits. And sneakers. Sneakers... that's why she didn't hear them approach.

"What... what the hell?" she asked, fighting the whimper in her voice.

The man in front, the oldest of the group, held a finger in the air to silence her. She could catch the glimpse of an expensive watch hanging loosely on his wrist beneath his cuff. Very expensive, like the suit, her mind immediately appraised. The man was wearing close to thirty grand in clothing and jewelry. Plus another grand for the automatic nestled in the side holster just visible beneath his jacket. This was no mugging or gang rape. Her stomach plunged... this was something infinitely worse.

"Attend, please, Sra. Lewis," he spoke in a cultured tone with only a faint trace of accent.

"What do you want?" she whispered, the sound barely escaping her lips.

The man lowered his finger and slowly ran his hand across the white stubble of goatee that ringed his mouth.

"We represent some former business associates of Sr. Jake Griffon. Sr. Griffon retained you as his attorney shortly before escaping from the Redwood Penitentiary. The men I represent are very anxious to locate Sr. Griffon and to… to speak with him."

The men behind him chuckled and muttered in Spanish.

"My clients are somewhat suspicious of your recent role in Sr. Griffon's life, especially with him being currently… how do you say? At large. Should you help to find him, they are willing to dismiss these suspicions."

He held her with a gaze that was both calm and predatory. She felt like a mouse being stared down by a very large cobra. The man handed her a business card.

"Here is a number in Mexico. If you should come across Sr. Griffon or gain any knowledge of his present location, you will call immediately, day or night."

Rachel moved to take the card, unable to keep her hand from trembling. She brushed it with her fingers, but the shaking came on stronger, and the card fluttered to the stained and cracked pavement. Her eyes widened and she moved to take a step back.

The man merely smiled and bent at the knees to pick up the card. He stood and handed it out to her again, smiling pleasantly as he did so. The men behind him snickered, and she saw one of them run his tongue slowly across his lips. She forced herself to reach for the card again, and the man pressed it firmly into her palm, holding her hand enfolded in his for a moment.

"Please Sra. Lewis. Make the call. Do not make me employ the full services of the men behind me. They are very experienced and very, ah... very committed to their work." He squeezed her hand. "Make the call."

She nodded her head slightly, her mouth an open O. The shakes were returning, starting deep in her core and working to her extremities. She fought internally for control.

The man nodded his head and turned on his heel. His companions turned and followed. Lewis watched as they continued down the street and climbed into a gleaming black Escalade with Baja plates. The engine purred to life and they drove slowly down the street. The shaking came on hard now, like a hurricane. She shook violently as she stood, her face a rictus of terror. Tears formed in the corners of her eyes, and suddenly her paralysis broke and she sprinted to the car, scrabbling madly for the keys.

Ripping open the door, she flung herself inside and slammed the door behind her, pressing the lock button. *Jesus, Jesus Fucking Christ*, she thought, *How? Fucking how? How did they know? And how in the Christ did they find her?* She grabbed the steering wheel with both hands and squeezed until her knuckles were white, fighting the shakes, tensing every muscle in her body. After a moment, she felt her muscles relax and the trembling subsided. *Good,* she thought, *good, ok.* She compelled herself to compartmentalize the terror and focus. It was time to get down to business. There was still time. Jesus Christ, please let there be enough time. She started the car and shot out from the curb, the scream of her engine echoing down the empty street like an animal at bay.

# CHAPTER 6

Greg Hollister leaned against the railing on his deck, a bottle of Fat Tire ale sweating in his palm, staring out over the lights of downtown LA in the distance. The setting sun cast reflections on the city's tall towers, like jewels shining in upright rectangular cases. This used to be his favorite time of day. *Sunset jewels*, his wife used to call them as they clinked glasses of wine and toasted the ending of the day. He couldn't remember the last time they shared that private toast.

The screen door whispered open behind him, and he sensed her moving closer.

"Hi, honey," she said sleepily, "I was just laying down with Tanner and didn't hear you come in. How long have you been home?"

"I don't know," he said listlessly, "a little while ago, I guess."

"I looked down from the bedroom window and saw you here. Are you ok? You haven't moved in ten minutes?"

"Just tired," he forced a smile on his face.

She moved up behind him and began to massage his shoulders.

"God, you're tense."

"Yeah. Just trying to figure a way out of this for all of us."

She turned him to face her, looking concerned and supportive.

"You've been working insane hours ever since this legal crap started. Can't they just give you back your inspector's license while it all gets sorted out? I mean, the inspection work wasn't killing you like this hands-on construction work." She smiled. "It's not like you robbed a bank or anything."

He forced the smile to stay on his face, but his eyes went blank.

"It just doesn't work that way, Cindy."

"If my brother can cut you in on something else, something like that prison construction job, will you take it? I mean, we hardly see you anyway, and it's guaranteed money."

He looked down at her. At Cindy. The woman he loved… or used to love, wasn't that right? What the hell happened? This was the woman he was planning to abandon with their son. It had all started like a dream that was rapidly spiraling into a nightmare. How the hell had things gone so far? Cindy with her innocence and trust and constant support. The very things that he thought were driving him insane that were now what he craved.

"I know," he said. "But my lawyer is down here and sooner or later that Long Beach job will work out."

She looked at him for a long moment, then placed the tips of her fingers on his cheeks and smiled.

He looked away, unable to bear her love, her so undeserved love.

"You know," he said drifting his gaze across the sloped yard, "I was standing here a few days back and I caught sight of this big old bird perched up on an aerial. Hard to believe someone around here still has one of those up, huh? Anyways, this was a big bird, a buzzard or something, and I remembered seeing him in that exact same position the day before. I started wondering if he was real or if he was stuffed. Like someone put a big stuffed buzzard up there to scare away pigeons or something. So I just stood here in the sun and watched him for the longest time, just watching until he flew away. Simple pleasures," he turned to say to her, "I miss the simple pleasures."

Cindy lifted herself on her tip toes and brushed her lips softly across his.

"I know a nice simple pleasure," she said. "Tanner should be down for the count and it's… it's been a long time."

He returned her kiss and slipped his arms around her, every nerve aching for relief and escape from the hell he had created. His hands slid down her back to cup her from behind, and as he opened his eyes, he saw his son standing in the sliding doorway, thumb in his mouth. Cindy followed his gaze and said, "Tanner, honey?"

The child stood, half asleep, and softly said, "Mommy, I dreamed about the monsters again."

She turned to approach him. "It's ok sweetie, Mommy's here." She paused and turned back to Hollister. "Sorry, honey," she shrugged.

She walked to the child and lifted him in her arms. As they entered the house, Hollister heard her say, "There's no such thing as monsters, sweetie."

He closed his eyes and dropped his head.   There were monsters, he knew.   Not the kind that Tanner thought were lying in wait under his bed or in his closet.   There were monsters who contemplated murder, who kidnapped, who abandoned their families. Oh, yes… there most certainly were monsters.

The ringing of his cell snapped him out of his self-loathing. He pulled it from his chinos and looked at the screen. *Christ, now what?* he thought, the anger rising like bile in him.   He swiped his finger across the screen and snapped, "What?"

"It's me," Lewis said in a rush, "Look we have to find him and now!  A couple of cartel heavies showed up and grabbed me on the street tonight.   They were fucking following me.   We're in big trouble, Greg."

He sighed. "Are you ok?"

"I'm fine for now, but I'm holed up in a hotel.   They've probably got my place staked out, and if they do, that's probably the only thing keeping Griffon from showing up there.  I can't go home until this thing is over.  I need your ear glued to the police scanner. If he shows up, the cops will be all over the air with it.   We have to get to him first."

"Fine," he said coldly, "If I hear anything, I'll call you."

Lewis paused, then said, "Good.   I'm at the Hyatt in Hollywood.  Ask for Sharon Jacobs."

"Did the Mexicans say anything about me?"

"No. If they develop an interest, believe me, you'll know."

"Great," he spat out. "How did this happen? I came to you a long time ago to help get my building inspector's license back, and now I've got cartel soldiers after me."

"*Listen!*" she shrieked into the phone, "Don't you fucking *dare* go soft on me now. You knew goddamned well what you were doing every step of the way. You're in this to the neck with me, and don't you fucking forget it! Just listen to the fucking scanner and call me if you hear anything." The connection clicked off.

Hollister stood, staring at the phone in his hand, feeling more impotent, more utterly hopeless than he ever had.

Back in her hotel room, Lewis threw the phone onto the bed and wrapped her fingers in her hair, squeezing. The very thing that had made Hollister so useful, the only thing, his puppy-dog eagerness to please her, was circling back around to bite her. She crossed to the mini bar and grabbed a palm-sized bottle of Johnny Walker Red, violently twisted off the cap, and drank it straight down. Tears welled up in her eyes as the liquor burned its way down her throat. She took a deep breath and walked back to the bed, picking up the phone and hitting the speed dial. After three rings, a voice said, "You have reached Special Agent David Goodwin at the Los Angeles Field Office of the Federal Bureau of Investigation. Please leave your name, number, and a brief message after the tone and I will get back to you."

She gulped several deep breaths of air before the message tone rang, then said in a breathless rush, "Agent Goodwin, this is Rachel Lewis. I called as soon as I could. I had to check into a hotel room, because I couldn't go home. Griffon called me at my office. He said he had been watching me and he saw me talking to you. He was crazy... ranting. I've dealt with a lot of insane clients in my time, but never like this. He said he was going to kill me and anyone else who got in his way. Including you. Please call me. I'm terrified. I'm at the Hollywood Hyatt under the name Sharon Jacobs. And please, be careful. I'm so sorry. Please call."

She hung up, and took a long, deep breath. A smile creased her face as she looked out the window where the rising moon hung suspended, a circle of bone in the slowly darkening sky.

## CHAPTER 7

The car's headlights lit up the drive, pooling around a small but immaculate adobe house on the end of a quiet, tree-lined street. Goodwin glanced somewhat mournfully at the home, then killed the engine and slipped the keys out of the ignition. As he exited the car, he turned to see Chiha already standing in the drive beside the car, looking off into the night. He had gotten out of the car and closed the door without making the slightest noise. Goodwin rubbed his eyes with the heels of his hands, blaming fatigue and preoccupation for his inattention.

He walked up the drive and unlocked the front door, pausing at the entrance to turn back. Chiha was still rooted to the driveway, eyes closed, face tilted up to the night.

"What are you doing?" he asked, wearily.

Chiha remained motionless for a moment, then spoke with his eyes still closed, "Listening."

Goodwin listened. There was no sound other than the faint drone of distant traffic and the gentle breath of wind through the trees.

"To what?"

Chiha opened his eyes. "That is the question."

Goodwin shook his head and trudged through the door, leaving it open behind him. He had just about all he could take of the strange man's eerie otherworldliness for one day. Dropping his briefcase on the hallway floor, he flipped on the light in the small living room. The room was so neat as to appear sterile, the only furniture spare and simple. A single picture hung on one of the amber walls.

He turned to see what was keeping Chiha only to yell out in surprise to see the man standing three feet from him in the room, staring intently at him.

"Christ!" he yelped. "Would you stop doing that?"

"Doing what?"

"The whole Indian Jim routine... the stoic silences, the sneaking up on me, the vague, prophetic answers... you're seriously starting to creep me out."

Chiha merely looked at him.

Goodwin sighed. "Look, I'm sorry. I don't mean to be offensive, but it's been one long goddamned day. I've just... I can honestly say I've never met anyone like you."

Chiha grinned, "I have heard that before."

Goodwin realized that this was the first attempt at humor he'd yet seen coming from the man, and he relaxed his bunched shoulders.

"Yeah, now *that* I can believe."

He gestured with his arm at the empty space of the living room and hall and said, "This place is really too big for me. But I had to get something that wouldn't remind me of where Sheryl and I lived. I wanted to show that I've moved on. There's only so much time you can spend at work. In the end, you have to go home sometime."

As he spoke, he removed his suit jacket and disappeared momentarily into the bedroom. Chiha watched as he returned and moved to the kitchen and opened the refrigerator. As he looked over the door of the fridge, Chiha noticed the shoulder holster still strapped to him.

"Can I get you something to drink?"

"Water."

Goodwin returned with a bottle of water in one hand and a Sam Adams in the other. He handed the water to Chiha, who looked at in for a moment as if mystified, then took it and unscrewed the top before taking a long swallow. Goodwin collapsed into a small, leather reading chair and motioned with his beer to the other doorways.

"Bathroom's there. There's a spare room, but I just use it for storage. I don't entertain a whole lot, so you're going to have to sleep on the couch. If you prefer the floor, I have an old sleeping bag around here somewhere."

He observed Chiha looking around uncomfortably.

"Different from a cabin in the woods, huh?"

Chiha fixed his gaze on him, a look of sadness crossing his face. "It is. This is not a home."

Goodwin paused with the beer bottle halfway to his lips.

"This is not your place, the place you go to feel most safe. It is not part of you and you are not part of it."

Goodwin felt the embarrassment rising, anger coming close on his heels. "Yeah, well, I didn't exactly see any family pictures hanging in your cabin."

Chiha was silent a moment, then closed his eyes. "There is no one for me to take pictures of."

Goodwin felt the anger dissipate, only to be replaced by a sheepish shame. He looked to the picture hanging centered over the small fireplace. Sheryl. He and Sheryl walking in the fall foliage in Northern Virginia. Sheryl with her face nearly as ruddy as the autumn leaves on that beautiful but chilly October day.

"Well... me neither, anymore."

He returned his attention to Chiha, who stood uncomfortably in the center of the room. The man just didn't seem to fit in anywhere. Not in this century, anyway. He wanted to change the subject, for things were hitting a little too morbidly close to heart.

"You never told me what happened to your family. How you came to be out in the middle of nowhere. Why no one has any record of your ever existing."

Chiha grew visibly uncomfortable.

"Look," Goodwin tried, "I know I'm not exactly in touch with my heritage, but it's strange to me that I've never heard of your people, and neither has anyone else."

Chiha answered, "You would not have known us by the name we called ourselves."

Goodwin felt his skin shiver as he noted the slight change in tone in the man's voice. The softness held the slightest hint of...

something. Chiha's hands were at his side, and his head was cocked at a slight angle.

"Your people," Chiha said in a whispery hiss, "would have called us the Long-Ears, or the *Hatcko-tcapko*."

"My people?" Goodwin asked, sensing something unpleasant gathering in the room. For no logical reason he could think of, he found himself wanting to move his hand closer to his shoulder holster.

"Your people... the Seminole. We have been called by many names by many nations... *Anuk Ite* to the Sioux, *Windigo* to the Ojibwe and Cree, *Shita* to the Hopi. Many names, none of them exactly correct."

"Why so many names?" Goodwin whispered across dry lips. The atmosphere in the room was changing, as though lightning were about to strike. He felt the fair hairs on his forearms rising. His fingers inched slightly closer to the grip of his pistol.

"Because," Chiha replied in a voice that was growing raspy. His eyes grew dark, as though drawing the light from the room like an animal, "People must give a name to what they most fear."

Then all Goodwin knew was a blur of movement. He never even saw Chiha move. Everything was chaos as something hard and muscled rammed him, knocking him across the room the same instant that the front window shattered, coughing safety glass on top of him like snowfall. He recovered himself in an instant, on his belly, gun already in his hand, sweeping the barrel across the room. He was alone. The sliding door into the back yard was open, and

Chiha was nowhere in sight. He shook the fragmented window glass from his hair and whipped his head from the shattered window to the wall across from it. A large hole, spiderweb cracks emanating from the center, sat in the wall at eye level. Where his head had been just before being driven to the ground by...

"*Shit!*" he yelled, looking for a blood trail, something to point him to Chiha's whereabouts. He rose to a crouch, weight balanced on the balls of his feet. A crashing in the bushes outside the window caused him to dive to the floor and roll away from his previous position, and he heard a round thud into the leather back of the chair. Then the air was filled with sounds unlike anything he had ever heard. A long, ululating animal scream that descended into a deep guttural growl raised the hairs on his neck. Then the sound of violent struggle, wild thrashings and a wet, ripping sound that ended in a hideous, meaty thud.

Goodwin crawled across the floor, dragging himself by his elbows, weapon pointed straight ahead. The hideous sounds from outside had subsided, and the silence was more unnerving. Reaching the sliding door, he righted himself to a sitting position, back to the metal door frame, and scanned the yard. Nothing moved. He tensed his leg muscles and broke for the cover of a ficus tree. Keeping the tree's thick trunk between himself and the back fence, he squatted on his heels and took several deep breaths, readying himself. He launched himself in a run, vaulting the low cedar fence, pushing himself up with his free hand to clear the top and hitting the ground in a roll. He was at the edge of the park that bordered his back yard, and he knew the terrain well. Without needing to look, he ran in a crouch for the stand of Hawthorne bushes at the park's edge and pulled up, sweeping his field of view with his gun. Nothing seemed out of place, but then he heard the rustling of branches coming from the thick wall of shrubs twenty yards to his right. He circled around to approach the shrubs from behind, staying low and keeping to the dark shadows. When nearly upon the mass of branches, he glanced up over the tops to see a clear line of sight to what used to be his living room window. Something was behind the first layer of shrubs, a dark shape crouched near the ground that seemed to vibrate. He heard a sound like tension cords stretching and snapping. On a silent three-count, he rose to a shooting stance, the Glock 22 feeling as secure in his hands as if it were a natural extension of his arm. He prepared to shout a warning and identification, but the words froze in his throat. The 9mm trembled slightly in his hands as he looked at what was staged in the open center of the shrubs like an unholy tableau.

Chiha stood slowly to face him, what remained of his clothes hanging in torn shreds about his sweat-slicked body. At his feet lay the remains of a man...or what used to be a man. One arm had been wrenched from the shoulder socket and lay several feet to the side, the hand still grasping the friction-taped grip of the sniper rifle. A ragged, gaping chunk had been taken out of his chest and throat, nearly severing the head, which still wore a frozen expression of surprise and horror. And Chiha stood, shoulders hunched over, his feet encoiled by the intestines spilling from the dead man's ruptured stomach. The air was chokingly heavy with the smell of blood and shit and a musky, animal odor. Chiha was breathing heavily, and for the first time, Goodwin saw his eyes. They were red, as if filled with blood, nearly bulging from their sockets. He was covered in blood, rivulets of which flowed from his mouth and spilled down over his chin, which was flecked with gore. Goodwin reflexively aimed his Glock at the center of Chiha's heaving chest and uttered, "Don't…don't move."

Chiha continued to pant heavily, but his eyes slowly dimmed, his irises returning to their normal flat brown. He opened his mouth and Goodwin felt his knees begin to buckle as he saw the massive size of the incisors, yellowed ivory with streaks of steaming red, gradually recede back into their gums. He steadied himself and said more forcefully, "Don't fucking move!" He steadied the trembling in his arms and sighted at center mass.

Chiha slumped slightly, a look of extraordinary weariness moving across his face, and said, "You must help me with the body."

Goodwin was stunned as if slapped across the face. None of this made sense, not even in the most remote sense of the term. He shook his head and applied more pressure to the gun's trigger.

"Don't you fucking move!"

Chiha nodded almost imperceptibly. "I am not armed. I had no choice. He was going to kill you." He moved his eyes to the sniper rifle, the finger of the severed arm still coiled about the trigger, then returned his gaze to Goodwin.

Goodwin wavered. The shattered window, the bullet holes, something knocking him down a second before the first shot hit the room. He kept his gun aimed squarely at the half naked man before him.

"You did it. You knocked me down. But how... this is... what the fuck are you?"

"I will explain later. We must move the body."

Goodwin felt rage come flooding up over his terror. "*Move the fucking body*? This is a crime scene...it's a goddamned slaughterhouse!" He removed one hand from his gun and reached for his cell, then remembering that he had taken his jacket off in the house. He was cut off from communication. "You put something in my drink, didn't you? Some kind of peyote shit that makes you see things. This... you..." he stopped, the horror taking control again.

"I saved your life. I will explain all in time. But we must move this man first. If I am in jail, you will be beyond saving. We are almost out of time to stop what is in motion." He looked with such great sorrow, that Goodwin took a reflexive step back. Then he added a single word filled with the sorrow of centuries. "Please."

# CHAPTER 8

The bar was crowded and the patrons were rowdy. Jake Griffon pushed his way through a sea of denim and leather to move up to the bar. He had spotted the tattered flier advertising the band up on stage blaring out what could laughably pass as music taped to a dilapidated fence on an empty side street earlier in the day. It was the name that caught his attention. Loup Garou. He had been hiding in alleys in the daylight, daring to use the bus only to get as far away from the safe house as he could before retreating into the shadows to await nightfall. Loup Garou. The words shouted out to him as he stood rooted to the sidewalk, sending him flashing back to the terror in the woods, images jump-cutting across his memory. It was what Batiste had whispered before... before what? There were too many blank spots in his memory tape.

He ripped the flier from the rotting wood with a shaking hand and crammed it into his pocket. Later, hidden behind a dumpster, he had taken it out and read the bar's name and address. The Sons of Leather. He had assumed it was a gay bar until he carefully approached after sunset, snaking his way through the shadow-filled alleys, to see what looked like a yuppie version of a biker bar. Big cruising BMWs and shiny new Harleys lined the street. A watering hole for weekend warrior bikers. Investment and management fucks who liked to play rough boy on their days off. Inside, it looked like a costume party: new leather jackets that had never been torn by chains or blades, denim cuts that had never been stained with blood.

He smiled. A supposed biker bar and not a neck tattoo or a patch in sight. He relaxed.

He looked across the bar at the mirror to see the reflected dance floor. It was crowded with people trying to dance to the band's bizarre hard rock version of the Cajun standard "Jolie Blonde."

He turned back to the bartender, a wispy thin Japanese woman with green-tinted hair and a rose tattoo coiling up from between her breasts, and shouted, "What's it mean?"

"What?" she shouted over the blaring music.

"What's it mean?" he asked more loudly.

She gave him an exasperated look. "What does *what* mean?"

"The band. Their name. What does it mean?"

"You got me. You want a drink or what?" she sniped.

Griffon smiled. "Black Jack. Three fingers."

The bartender gave him a brief, appreciative look and turned to get a bottle from the top shelf. He felt a warm hand slide over his own and flinched, turning quickly to see a very tipsy woman in skintight acid washed jeans and a flannel shirt tied across her considerable midriff. She was a good ten years older than him, a little large for his liking, and her sun-wrinkled face had all of the appeal of tanned leather, but it *had* been a long stretch in prison. He grinned.

"A little jumpy there, sweetie. It's just little old me," she giggled drunkenly.

He shrugged his shoulders, allowing his gaze to travel down

the valley of her considerable cleavage, allowing her to notice him looking.

"Werewolf," she said.

Griffon stiffened. "*What?*" he hissed, grasping her hand.

She wrenched her hand from his. "Easy, sugar." She shook her hand, which was smarting from his grip. "I ain't into that rough stuff." She leaned in and whispered, "Not out here in public, anyway." She tried to wink, but the effect was more of a twitch.

"What did you mean?" he asked, regaining control of himself.

"The band. Loup Garou. It's Cajun. Means werewolf. I watch all them monster documentaries on cable. Loup Garou, the Lizard Man, Skunk Ape, The Beast of Bray Road." She paused and steadied herself against the bar. "If you want to know 'bout monsters, I'm your gal."

"Cajun... werewolf?" Griffon asked.

"You got it, honey. Some kind of swamp witch curse that turns men into werewolves that go out howlin' in the swamp and tearin' folk up."

"Well," he said with a widening grin, "This does seem like a night to howl at the moon."

He took the aging barfly by the hand, his eyes never leaving hers, and led her onto the dance floor. They danced closely, bodies grinding against each other in the sea of people. Griffon felt himself begin to stiffen as the woman ground her pelvis firmly into his.

"Oh, my Sugar," she slurred, "I guess the full moon really

does bring out the beast in you."

Griffon felt more alive than ever, his nerve endings firing rapidly, he could smell every scent in the bar: the booze, the sweat, the grease from the fryer in the back kitchen, perfume and cologne, leather and denim. It was like mainlining odor. His body began to itch as if he had rolled in a patch of poison ivy. The drunken woman was pushing her face up for a kiss, her tongue emerging from her scarlet lips. Griffon smelled the whiskey on her breath, felt the heat from her mouth, could almost taste the saliva on her tongue…

Then he was hit from behind, knocked forward a step. A sticky wetness ran down his back. He whirled to see a young man in a leather jacket, eyes glazed with alcohol, an empty beer stein in his hand.

"Jesus… sorry, bro," the man slurred, looking at his empty glass, "So sorry dude… aw, man, I spilled my beer."

Griffon stood rooted to the dance floor, staring hard at the man, breathing in deep breaths. The man looked into his eyes and took a step back. The eyes were more than intense, they were… alive, on fire, tinges of red and orange coloring the irises.

"Whoah, whoah, dude… it was an accident. I'm sorry… hey, let me buy you a drink," he said, hands raised in supplication.

The woman looked at Griffon, and concern crossed her face.

"Hey, Sugar, don't get all alpha-male, it's ok. I'll just take you somewhere where we can get that wet shirt off you." She reached up to touch his shoulder, but Griffon whirled around to her, and she backed off, one wrinkled hand rising to her mouth.

"Jesus... Jesus what the hell?" she stammered, pierced by Griffon's fiery eyes and the snarl that had reshaped his face.

Griffon sensed movement behind him and rapidly turned to see the man behind him backing away. His body moving on animal instinct, Griffon lashed out and caught the man with a backhand across his chest that sent him flying across the room, bowling over several people on the dance floor. He sensed movement to his right, and saw two huge bouncers trying to make their way to him, hampered by the patrons trying to run from the floor. He opened his mouth and let out an animal growl that caused the bouncers to pause in their advance. In the shadows, his face began to ripple, and his shirt tore at the biceps. The bouncers collected themselves and rushed towards him.

As the larger one neared, Griffon lashed out and the man reeled back, blood flying from his throat in an arterial spray. Griffon leapt backwards, bounding like an animal, and landed on the bar, where he kicked out and sent the other bouncer crashing into the wall. He looked around the room in a low crouch, a guttural growl emanating from his throat. The band had stopped playing, and the crowd was staring in horror at the carnage on the floor. He sensed movement to his left, and swung his head to see the bartender talking frantically on the phone. He looked to the exit and leapt over the heads of several astonished patrons, then scrambled out the door and into the alley, careening off a dumpster before fleeing into the night.

# CHAPTER 9

Goodwin tried to pour himself a whiskey, but his hands shook so badly that he managed to spill as much onto the kitchen counter as in his glass. Chiha emerged from the bathroom, his face still wet from washing. Goodwin took a long pull from the glass and forced himself to look at the figure in the doorway.

"You've got to be fucking kidding me," he said in a harsh voice. He glanced to the pistol next to the bottle.

Looking at the bottle, Chiha sighed and said, "That will not help you. For this, you need a clear head." He walked slowly to the wall facing Goodwin and sat down against it, legs crossed.

"For what?"

Chiha said nothing for a long moment, seeming to look deeply within himself. "I have no wish to harm you. I need your help to find this man Griffon and right what I have done. But first, I must make you understand why this is so. I must tell you the story of my people.

"In the beginning, when the Creator made man, he saw that he had made a creature that had powers unlike any other. Man could do great good; he could also do great evil. To keep man humble, to show him he could not use the Earth and its creatures as he pleased, the creator made the ChaHo. We were made like men but if roused to anger, we could change our bodies into those of the great beasts, swifter and stronger than man's great warriors. The creator told the ChaHo to love the Earth and to protect it with our lives. We were not to use our power for conquest, so the Creator made us few, but whenever we saw men turn to evil, we were to cut that evil with our teeth and claws to purify the Earth.

"To guard against our using this power carelessly, the Creator made it that if we drew blood without killing the man, then the human would turn. He would become a creature that would mock the existence of the ChaHo. Such a half-blood would have no control over his shifting, he would be wracked with pain and fever at the time of the full moon. Then, drunk with the power to kill, he would exist only to do evil. The half-blood could exist unknown among men until the coming of the next moon. His savagery would turn all men against us.

"So the ChaHo sought to live at the edges of the world and to be cautious with our power. But still, man saw our power and grew jealous. They feared we would rule over them. They rose against us and there was war. The ChaHo, being few, were hunted. When the great ice mountains came from the north and the land bridge rose from the sea, the remaining ChaHo fled to the new land and hid in new places. The men who followed us found a land rich in the abundance of the Creator's gifts. They used the land wisely, which was good, for there were too few of us to stop them. They came to accept us as just another tribe, and we became part of their legends. We grew fewer and fewer."

ChaHo paused and closed his eyes. Goodwin sat, the drink frozen in his hand.

"When the white men came to the new land, they changed

the very Earth. They came in numbers greater than the stars and they brought with them terrible new weapons and sickness that burned through the tribes like fire through straw. The ChaHo knew we could not stand against them, and we fled to the furthest places. The whites brought with them half-forgotten memories of the ChaHo, twisted into legends in which they saw only their own savagery in us. For their fear of these legends, they slaughtered the wolves of the forest, thinking they were us. A few of us moved to their cities and tried to fit in to the white world, but they sickened and died.

"The rest thought we were safe in the forests of the West, but in the end, the whites came even there. Some of them built a village in the hills a few miles from ours. These were men so violent and so filled with hate that their own elders feared and shunned them. But we did not know this until it was too late.

One day, they found one of us. They shot her in the woods and cut off her hair, leaving her body for the crows. The next night, the ChaHo came to their village while the whites were sleeping and in our rage, we slaughtered everyone we found. I do not know how my forefathers thought such an act could end, because soon the soldiers came. Men from other tribes led them to us. They surrounded the village at dawn and began shooting. When it was over, they dragged the bodies to the great lodge and burned it to the ground. Some of my people were away from the village that day, or the story of the ChaHo would have ended there. When my forefathers returned they found only ashes and bone. Fourteen summers ago, I returned my father to the Earth. I am the last of the ChaHo."

Goodwin set his glass down. Neither man moved, sitting in the silence of the dark room.

"Well," Goodwin said, breaking the silence, "it may take you a while, but once you start talking, you tell one hell of a story."

Chiha said nothing.

Goodwin sighed. "I found records of the army sending an expedition into the area, but there was nothing about its mission."

"Who would keep records of such an act? The whites were tired of fighting the tribes. They thought they had conquered them all. What happened in the white village was an embarrassment to them. After the soldiers left, no more white men came to the area until the building of the prison. I had hoped to die before they came again." Chiha paused. "Now I know it would have been best if I had."

"What happened that night? The night the prisoners came to your cabin?"

Chiha looked pained, shrinking inward as he spoke, "I saw white men with guns come to my home. I should have let them just pass on, but I saw in them the soldiers who killed my people, and I was filled with hate. I would have killed you had you been there that night. There seemed no choice. Because of my rage and my foolishness, the power that was entrusted to us is now in the hands of an evil man. He does not know what he will become, and the legends of his own people will confuse him. He will become sick and will see the changes in his body that will come and go, growing stronger as the moon nears full. Then he will shift. He will have the strength of a great beast, but his heart will remain black. He will become overwhelmed with the urge to do great violence. That is why I have come here. I must help you find this man and right the evil I have done. A pure blood is dangerous only when he is enraged. This man will kill whenever he wants. He will kill until he is killed."

Goodwin held the man's sorrowful but determined gaze for a long moment, then stood, holstering his sidearm. He slipped into his jacket and said, "Come on."

"Where are we going?" Chiha asked.

"To my office. I'm going to show you everything we have on Griffon."

"Then... you believe."

Goodwin turned. "I don't know what I believe right now. But I sure as hell believe that considering what just happened out there, I'll feel better with you in my sight."

Chiha extended his legs and pushed himself from the floor. Goodwin's phone rang out.

"Agent Goodwin," he said into the cell, then listened for a few moments. He shot a glance over at Chiha. "I'll be right over."

Chiha raised his eyebrows.

"Change of plans. We're heading over to Long Beach."

Chiha opened his mouth to speak, but Goodwin beat him to the punch: "Some bar in Long Beach. They spotted him. Let's go."

128

# CHAPTER 10

Goodwin sped through the night, weaving in and out of traffic as Chiha gripped the dashboard tightly, his face expressionless.

"He will be gone before we get there."

Goodwin kept his eyes on the road, scanning for gaps between the cars as he blew past.

"Probably good. Forgot my silver bullets, anyway."

"That is part of your mythology. If you shoot him in the head or heart, he will die the same as you. The type of bullet is not important."

"You can be killed like that?"

Chiha considered.

"It is not easy. On your own, he will kill you before you even get to fire. He is as intelligent as you, but faster and stronger than you can imagine. But even a pure blood can be killed if wounded badly enough. We heal faster and can survive wounds that could kill a man, but we are mortal."

"So you can kill him?"

"Yes, as he can kill me. But neither of us will get the chance to kill the other if we cannot find him. In the forest, I can track him anywhere. In this city ... it is more difficult. I cannot find him without you."

Goodwin pulled a hard right from the far left lane, leaving the squeal of tires and angry honking of horns in his wake.

"We're stuck with each other, then."

"It would appear so."

. . .

Goodwin pulled up sideways in front of the Sons of Leather. Police cars and two ambulances blocked the right lane. Officers were questioning bar patrons and keeping onlookers at bay in the flashing red lights. A large man dressed in a shirt emblazoned with the bar logo sat on the curb while a young paramedic tended to a gash on his head while a patrolman took notes. Goodwin listened in as he approached.

"I wouldn't believe me either, man. But you didn't see his face. Ask anyone, man." He swept his arm to the shell-shocked witnesses huddled in groups on the sidewalk. "He jumped backwards on the bar like a fuckin' cougar, then jumped halfway across the fuckin' room. An' his face … it fuckin' changed, man. There some new drug on the street? 'Cause whatever it is, count me fuckin' out."

The paramedic and the cop exchanged glances.

"C'mon guy. You got a concussion." He helped the bouncer to his feet. "We'll get you checked out, okay?"

Goodwin looked at Chiha. The paramedic walked the bouncer to the ambulance and helped him inside. Goodwin walked over to the detective, holding up his ID card.

"Special Agent Goodwin. This was Jake Griffon?"

"We don't know exactly. The description that was called in fits, but then we show up and we got wits giving us conflicting descriptions of his face. All we know is the guy was leaping around the bar like Superman, took out three guys, jumps on the bar, then hightails it out the back door. One in the morgue, two in the hospital. We got cars combing the area looking for him."

"How long's he been gone?"

"Maybe twenty minutes."

"Shit. Clothes?"

The detective flipped back a few pages in his notebook.

"Jeans. Sweatshirt. Baseball cap. No one's sure of the colors. You know how it goes."

"Thanks." Goodwin turned to leave.

"Sure. One other thing though."

Goodwin turned back to him.

"People think he was on some new kind of drug. Not just because of how he moved, but because his face ... shit, I don't believe this myself."

"What about his face?"

"They said his face was ... rippling. That's their word, not mine. Rippling like waves. Fuckin' crazy, huh?"

Goodwin said nothing, grabbing Chiha by the arm and steering him towards the bar.

"He ran out the back about twenty minutes ago. The cops have a rough description and are looking for him. From what they told me about his movements and energy, he's probably sprinted to the city limits by now."

"No. He will be tired."

"What?" Goodwin asked, pulling him to a stop.

"When he becomes angry or frightened, he has already begun to change. But after, he will be weak. He will feel sick almost to the point of death. He may be close by, hiding until his strength returns. If we find him soon, he will be easier to take."

"That's great, but if the cops get to him first, they won't know what they've got."

"Take me into this building where he was fighting."

"Why?"

"I can track him."

"This is the city. There won't be any tracks to follow."

"I don't mean footprints." The irises of his eyes grew slightly larger, and his nostrils flared.

"Fine," Goodwin hissed and steered him towards the bar.

Inside, a forensics unit was busy searching for evidence, anything that would positively identify Griffon as the instigator of the violence earlier that night. The band's equipment was still on stage, the instruments laying where they had been dropped in the panic that set in once Griffon, if in fact it was him, had let loose. Goodwin steered Chiha to the bar.

"According to the witnesses, he jumped up on here before fleeing out the back. Apparently, he's not too..."

He trailed off, staring open-mouthed at Chiha, who lowered his head a few inches off the bar top. He took a long, slow breath in through his nose and held it. From the other side of the room, the forensics people stopped what they were doing to stare. Chiha exhaled and moved towards the back door.

"I know," he said.

"Know what?"

Chiha didn't acknowledge the question, moving purposefully to the door. Goodwin followed as he pushed open the door and walked into the dark alley behind the bar. Chiha paused, holding up one hand. Goodwin stopped, opened his mouth to repeat the question, then closed it. Chiha slowly rotated his head from right to left, bent at the knees, and squatted on his haunches.

"You know what?" Goodwin asked again, irritated.

Chiha stood to his full height and peered into the darkness at the east side of the alley.

"It was him. I know which way he went."

The back door banged open and one of the forensic team stepped into the alley.

"Who the hell are you guys?"

Goodwin held up his ID.

The man looked at the ID, then to Goodwin, and finally to Chiha.

"I know you're a fed, but that guy sure the hell isn't. What's he…"

"He's with me. Get back inside and do your damn job. Every minute you waste asking dumb questions, Griffon gets farther away."

The forensic man blustered, "Yeah, but he isn't supposed to be in here."

Goodwin strode up inside his personal space, jamming the ID under his nose.

"This tells you all you need to know. The Bureau's running this one, and I don't have time for lab geek bullshit. I said he's with me. Now get the fuck back inside."

The forensic man stammered and blushed, then retreated back into the bar, no doubt headed for one of the detectives.

"I hope you know the hell what you're doing," Goodwin said as Chiha walked off down the alley and into the night.

. . .

Griffon stumbled along a walkway between two stucco apartment complexes before collapsing against a wall between two garbage cans. He hugged himself as tremendous pain ripped through his body, falling to his knees in white-hot agony. He rolled across the pavement and under a hedge on the far side of the walkway, lying there as the spasms rolled over him like ocean waves. A light pinning the walkway caused him to raise his head and look out between the low branches of the hedge.

A patrol car cruised by on the street, the passenger sweeping the area between the two buildings with the car's searchlight. Hidden beneath the hedge, Griffon watched as the car drove past, then rolled out from under the hedge and propped his back against the wall.

He stared at his right hand, breath coming in jagged gasps, and tried to move his fingers. Sweat popped on his forehead from the exertion, but all he could manage was a feeble twitching of his fingertips. He slammed his hand against his thigh repeatedly in frustration, then looked to the sky. The moon that had just broken through the patchy clouds was almost full.

# CHAPTER 11

Hollister sat in his pickup in a strip mall parking lot, taking long pulls from a bottle of Stoli's wrapped in a brown paper bag. He knew he was more drunk than he felt, his body well on its way to intoxication, but his mind clear and running on overdrive. *Goddamn bitch is going to get me killed yet.*

Just a short while ago, he had been eating Fritos and listening to the police scanner in the front seat of his pickup near Bixby Park. He spilled the snacks all over the cab seats when a burst of static came over the scanner followed by an all-car alert.

*... disturbance at Sons of Leather bar off Broadway and Cerritos. Multiple injuries. Suspect fitting description of Jake Griffon on foot in the area. Suspect considered armed and extremely dangerous. All cars...*

He cut the scanner and fumbled for his cell phone.

"Hello?" Lewis asked nervously.

"It's me."

For Christ's sake I told you not to..."

"Shut up. They found him."

"*What*? Where?"

"Sons of Leather off Cerritos and Broadway. There was some kind of trouble there, and the cops think our boy started it."

"They have him in custody?"

"No. Sounds like they're still looking, but they mentioned him by name. There's an all-car..."

"*Fuck.* Meet me a block north on Cerritos and Appleton. We'll use your car. If it's him, there's a chance we can snatch him before the cops do."

"Are you crazy? Do you know the odds of our finding him? Every cop in the city is rolling."

"The odds are shitty and getting shittier every minute we waste talking about them. Fucking *drive*, damn it! I'll be there in fifteen."

So here he sat, drinking up his courage. Headlights swung into the lot and the Porsche screeched to a stop beside him. Rachel got out, locked her car with the remote, then opened the truck door and slung herself up in the seat next to him. The spilled Fritos crunched under her as she sat, and she made a disgusted face as she surveyed the mess in the cab. She eyed the paper bag nestled in his crotch.

"Jesus, are you *drunk?* Drunk now?"

"No. I just needed a slug to steady my nerves."

"Get out. I'm driving. The last thing we need is for you to get popped for a DUI. Shit-fuck me, there are cops all over the streets, you idiot."

"If you don't want to ride with me, then why not take two cars? We can cover more area."

Rachel leaned back and slapped him hard across the face. Hollister put a hand to his cheek, his eyes watering.

"Listen numbnuts, you want to try to subdue him on your own? Because I sure don't. I'll drive and you keep your eyes on the streets. Have the gun?"

"In the glove box."

Rachel opened the compartment and withdrew the small automatic. She pulled back the slide and jacked a round into the chamber.

"At least you didn't fuck that part up. Now get out and sit over here."

Hollister got out and slunk over to enter from the passenger door as Rachel slid over and started the truck, pulling out of the lot and into traffic.

They cruised in silence, Hollister scanning the streets as she drove. A police car passed in the oncoming lane, and Lewis watched nervously until it receded in the rear-view mirror. The silence was broken only by the occasional burst of patter from the police scanner. Another patrol car swung in behind them and rode their bumper for two blocks before turning right onto a side street. Lewis let out the breath she had been holding.

"That's the second one in less than a minute."

Rachel looked up the block to a man sitting at a bus stop. His arms were wrapped around his waist as he rocked slowly back and forth.

"I can count. Neither car had their rollers on. If they find him, we'll know."

She pulled the truck to a stop at the corner as the figure on the bench rocked off his seat and lay on the sidewalk. The streetlight hit his face. The face clicked with Lewis.

"It's him!"

She cut a hard right onto the cross street and slammed to a stop at the curb, tucking the gun into the waistline of her pants as she scrambled from the truck. She bent on one knee next to Griffon as Hollister walked unsteadily to stand next to her. Lewis shook Griffon by the shoulder.

"Hey, asshole."

Griffon propped himself on one elbow and stared glassily at her, pale and shaking. He rolled onto his side and vomited bile onto the sidewalk.

"Christ, what are you on?"

"Can we just get out of here, please?" Hollister asked, noticing the disgusted looks of people passing by on the sidewalk.

Lewis unbuttoned her jacket to show Griffon the gun.

"See this? You're coming with us, or God help me I'll shoot you right here."

Together, she and Hollister hauled Griffon to his feet and hustled him over to the truck, depositing him in the back seat of the extended cab. Rachel got in beside him, the gun now in her hand.

"You drive," she said to Hollister. "Just keep it slow, and for Christ's sake don't get pulled over. I have cuffs in my car. Drive there and I'll follow you back to the house."

Hollister got behind the wheel and pulled out into traffic. As he turned right to loop back to Rachel's car, Chiha rounded the corner of an alley and approached the bus stop, followed by Goodwin. He knelt in front of the bench, feeling the spot where

Griffon had lain seconds before. He closed his eyes and inhaled deeply. After a long moment, he opened his eyes and looked at Goodwin.

"He was here. Others were with him. Perhaps two. They walked there," he said, pointing to the side street, "then there is nothing."

Goodwin looked from the bench to the curb of the cross street, then hung his head, rubbing the heels of his hands against his eyes in frustration.

. . .

Griffin slumped in a wooden chair, hands cuffed behind his back, his head resting on his chin. A brutal slap from Rachel rocked his head violently to the side. He tilted his head slowly and stared at her, his face still pale. His shakes had stopped.

"We're out of time here, asshole. You're sick, but there are no marks on your arms so you haven't shot up. It must be your infection, and believe me Jake, I will let you rot from the inside out and die if you don't give up the stones. The cops are all over the city looking for you, so it's now or never time."

"I give them up ... you cap me."

"You're going to die anyway if you don't get medical help, so what's to lose? Give me the stones and we're gone. I'll call the cops from the airport and tell them you're here." She leaned in close to his face. "Live or die, Jake. Your choice."

Griffon looked from Lewis to Hollister, who was standing in the doorway with the gun pointed shakily at him. He looked at the gun.

"Inside a cinderblock wall in Carson."

"*Where* in Carson?"

Griffon considered for a moment.

"Southwest corner of Del Amo and Willington. West end of the wall."

"Why didn't you just grab them yourself tonight?" she asked, suspicious.

Griffon chuckled and spat a wad of bloody phlegm on the floor.

"You'll see when you get there."

Rachel kept her eyes locked on Griffon.

"*I'm* not going anywhere. Greg, you go check this out. I'll stay and keep Mr. Griffon here company."

"You think he's setting us up?"

"Maybe."

"So how come I have to go?" Hollister whined.

"Because the last time I left you in charge here, he escaped. Now give me the goddamned gun and get going."

Hollister bristled. "If you don't trust me then maybe you should ask yourself why I don't just grab the diamonds and keep on going? I mean, what are you going to do? Call the cops?"

Rachel turned to fix him with a stare that was cold steel.

"No, Greg, I'm not going to call the cops. I'll just call Los

Zetas and tell them who has their diamonds and let them handle it. Even if they don't get to you first, they'll certainly find wifey and your boy. I do that and you'd better pray the cops get to you and them first. Ever see how they interrogate people? Not a pretty sight, Greg. They let their chainsaws do the talking."

Hollister looked at her in shock for a long moment. She had never threatened Cindy and Tanner before. He didn't think even she could play so dirty, but her look convinced him.

"Fuck you, and I guess I'll see you later."

"Good boy. Don't fuck this up, and we'll be on that beach before you know it. Now hand me the gun."

Hollister struggled with the thought of turning the gun on her and ending this madness now. He twitched. He screwed up courage. Then he collapsed inwardly and handed the automatic to her. He turned without comment and hustled to his truck. *Goddamn but you're a coward. Why didn't you shoot her when you had the chance?* He played that mental track on a loop all the way to Carson.

# CHAPTER 12

The interior of the FBI Field Office was brightly lit despite the small number of people working in offices and cubicles. Goodwin led Chiha to his office and closed the door behind them.

"Take a seat. I'll show you everything we have on Griffon. Tell me if anything clicks. It's all I can think of now. It's late, and I'm out of ideas."

He went to his desk and switched on the computer with one hand while playing back his phone messages with the other. He skipped through several inter-departmental messages, then Rachel Lewis's voice came on:

*Agent Goodwin, this is Rachel Lewis. I called as soon as I could. I had to check into a hotel room, because I couldn't go home. Griffon called me at my office. He said he had been watching me and he saw me talking to you. He was crazy... ranting. I've dealt with a lot of insane clients in my time, but never like this. He said he was going to kill me and anyone else who got in his way. Including you. Please call me. I'm terrified. I'm at the Hollywood Hyatt under the name Sharon Jacobs. And please, be careful. I'm so sorry. Please call.*

Goodwin replayed the message.

"Why is Griffon starting a bar fight in Long Beach if he's planning on coming after me?" He looked at Chiha. "Why don't I

143

believe a word of that?"

"Perhaps we should go help this woman."

Goodwin picked up the desk phone and punched in a number.

"They don't have lawyers where you're from, do they? Hi, yes. I need the number for the Hollywood Hyatt ... Thank you, and please connect me ... Hi, can you connect me to Sharon Jacobs, please? ... What time? This is Special Agent David Goodwin with the FBI ... No, there's no trouble, thanks."

He turned to Chiha.

"She checked out this morning. I have her business card here somewhere." He rummaged around in his desk drawer and pulled out the card. He was about to dial, but paused when he saw Chiha staring intently at the card. Chiha rose from his chair and gently reached across the desk to take Goodwin's hand and move the card closer to his nose. The hand that held his wrist felt rough and dry, like sandpaper. Chiha inhaled and looked at Goodwin.

"She is one of the people with Griffon at the bus stop."

Goodwin shuddered involuntarily.

"You're sure?"

Chiha nodded.

Goodwin punched three numbers on the phone.

"Heather, Dave Goodwin. I need a home address for a Rachel Lewis. That's L-E-W-I-S. Local attorney with an office at 22976 Wilshire. Great. Call me back with the info on my cell. I'll be driving."

He hung up and looked at Chiha.

"Come on. This doesn't feel right."

They left the office and jogged to the front door, urgency driving them like a rushing wind.

. . .

Griffon sat upright in the chair, staring intently at Rachel, who returned his glare from her seat across the room. His returning vitality spooked her, especially coming back as quickly as it did. She held the gun propped on her crossed legs, the barrel aimed at his chest. He could smell her fear rising from her and wafting across the room like ripe body odor.

"You know," he grinned, "if things had been different, I think you would have been interesting to get to know."

"Yeah? Well I'm not in the mood for banter, so just keep your mouth shut and hope that he comes back with those diamonds, okay?"

"That's not really my problem. For someone so creative, I mean putting this whole thing together, you lack imagination. You just can't look beyond the everyday world. You have no curiosity."

"Jesus, you did get high, didn't you? You're rambling. Delirious."

"You want to see something curious, Rachel?"

"What I want is for you to shut the fuck up." She raised the gun.

"Come on, don't you even wonder how I broke out of here? Now that made *me* curious at the time. Of course, my perspective has changed since."

"If I were you, I'd be more curious about luck … especially how yours is running out by the second."

"Yes. Yes, I guess you're right about luck. But it wasn't lucky for you to send him off after the diamonds now, was it?"

Rachel rose from the chair, her arms rigid as she pointed the gun.

"Shut the fuck up, or I swear I'll put a bullet through your fucking heart."

"Rachel, Rachel. You have such an unimaginative view of the world. All you see here is a man cuffed to a chair. I think it's time I awakened your curiosity."

Griffon closed his eyes and rolled his head in slow circles. He gritted his teeth and hunched his back, flexing the muscles in his arms and torso. A loud metallic snap sent Rachel stumbling back a few feet, the gun wavering in her hands. Griffon slowly raised his arms, the broken chain of the handcuffs dangling from his wrists.

"Curious, Rachel?"

"*What the fuck*? Sit back down. Goddamn it, sit down or I'll shoot!"

The shaking in her hands increased.

"Relax, Rachel. The show's just beginning. You have so much to learn."

She steadied the gun and began squeezing the trigger. He

moved so fast that she didn't even see it happen. The gun flew across the room, and a sharp pain rocketed up her hand.

Griffon was standing two feet away, grinning.

She looked to her hand and saw that her index finger was missing, torn from the socket and squirting blood. She staggered back, gripping her wounded hand. Across the room, the automatic lay on the floor, her severed finger still hooked in the trigger guard. She looked back to Griffon, who looked taller somehow. She watched in horror as he raised his impossibly long fingers to his mouth and licked the blood from them. *Her* blood.

She bolted for the door to the kitchen. As she reached the threshold, she slammed into Griffon and bounced back a step. He stood with his arms calmly folded across his chest. Her brain refused to register how he could move so fast and tilted into full panic mode. She screamed and ran to the back of the room, staring at him from behind the chair with bugged-out eyes.

"Where do you think you'll go, Rachel? This is just the warm-up. You still have so much to learn."

She grabbed the chair and rushed him, screaming as she swung the chair in a strong arc towards his head. Griffon remained still until the last second, then the chair shattered against his suddenly upraised arm. He reached out and took Rachel's wrists in his hands, now grown coarse and prickly.

"So strong, Rachel. You don't give up. I can appreciate that. If only things had been different."

He stepped backwards into the kitchen, pulling her with him.

"Come on. Let's get this party started."

She moved her mouth rapidly, but no words came. Pulling against him was futile. Digging in her heels had no effect either, as he simply pulled her along as if she were on rollers.

The kitchen was lit and the police scanner gleamed on the counter next to a small radio. He released one of Rachel's hands and hit the power switch, killing the scanner in mid-squawk. He turned on the radio, fiddling with the tuner until he found a rock station. He turned up the volume as the Rolling Stones began "Gimme Shelter."

"Let's dance."

He pulled her close to him and she nearly gagged on the musky smell rolling off him. He pinned her wrist behind her back and began grinding himself against her, swaying in time to the music. She closed her eyes and shook in helpless terror as he moved his head down and sniffed her neck, his exhales hot and putrid against her skin.

"You know, Rachel," he said, his voice low and raspy, "they talk about the smell of fear. If they only knew how intoxicating it really is."

He released one wrist and traced a line down the side of her throat with a sharp nail. She squirmed in his embrace, feeling behind her back with her free hand for the box cutter near the sink. Her finger brushed the cutter when she felt herself spinning across the room. Her back slammed against the refrigerator hard enough to rattle the shelves inside.

He was on her in less than a second, one hand crushing her

throat. The grip was like a steel band and then she felt herself lifted, feet kicking in the air. Griffon held her six inches off the ground as he calmly walked to the door to the back yard, holding her in front of him, humming along to the song.

He carried her by the throat into the backyard. Black spots danced in her vision as the lack of oxygen took its toll.

"Ok, Rachel. Enough foreplay. Time for the main event. It's show time."

His face twitched and rippled, nostrils flaring as his breathing quickened. His eyes never leaving hers, his lips drew back in hideous mockery of a grin, revealing teeth that had grown longer and more yellowed.

Rachel opened her mouth to scream, but all that escaped Griffon's steel grip was a feeble croak. She watched in horror as the skin of his face rolled and rippled, reshaping his features. The bones under the skin shifted, altering his features beneath the writhing flesh. His eyes grew larger and took on an orange color as muscles popped up from nowhere on his arms and chest.

"I have to say," he said through a mouth crammed with oversized teeth, "I do believe I'm getting better at this."

He released his grip, and Rachel dropped to the ground like a sack. She gulped in great gasps of air, rolling onto her back. Towering over her, what used to be Jake Griffon stood erect and raised his shaggy arms to the night sky, backlit by the orange moon. As he bent to her, arms outstretched, she finally uttered a long, piercing scream that was abruptly cut off. The neighborhood dogs barked frantically, shattering the still night as a new kind of predator moved in for the kill.

# CHAPTER 13

A flashlight beam played across the shelves of a bookcase from the sliding doors that led to the back patio. On the shelf, framed photos of Rachel Lewis reflected back the glare. Rachel riding a bicycle as a child. A high school graduation. Reading a law book in student housing. A mangy Australian shepherd with two tennis balls in its mouth. Law school graduation in cap and gown. The flashlight beam moved across the room, revealing expensive mission-style furniture upon which stacks of folders, coffee mugs, and dirty plates were scattered.

On the back patio, Goodwin and Ciha stood on a deck set above a small, but lushly vegetated garden. Behind them, a wooden Adirondack chair and small round table sat, covered with a thick layer of dust. Goodwin turned from the sliding door.

"Nothing. I have to break in to be sure, though."

"Why?"

"She might be hiding upstairs."

"There is no one in the house."

"How do you know?"

"Her scent here is old. She has not been here in days. There is no sound in the house. There is no one here."

Goodwin stared at him for a moment and shrugged.

"Fine. I'm on shaky ground here without a warrant, anyway."

They walked in silence to the car. Chiha paused to look at the hunter's moon hovering over the city lights down the hills from where they stood. He looked from the desert willow and manzanita on the hillsides to the urban sprawl below. A song began in his mind, sung long ago when he was a very young child. He shook himself out of the past and heard Goodwin ending a phone conversation.

"Her car's not here either. Find out what she drives and call me back. No, don't sweat the protocol. Got her voicemail saved. I'll log it later. Get everyone on this now, but prioritize the car. Right. Thanks."

Goodwin returned his cell to his vest pocket and opened the driver's door.

"What do we do now?" Chiha asked.

"We hope they find her, then hope she leads us to Griffon.

"Hope?"

"Yeah," Goodwin sighed, "believe it or not, we do a lot of that around here."

# BLOOD MOON

# CHAPTER 1

Water ran down the bathroom sink drain, stained red and then pink before finally running clear. Griffon splashed water on his face, clearing away spots of blood and bits of flesh and hair. He ran handfuls of water over his hair, slicking it back with his fingers before looking into the mirror over the sink. He turned his head from left to right, mesmerized by the return of normalcy to his features, then wiped the sink clean with his hands before turning off the water.

He grabbed a towel off the bar mounted to the wall and glanced at the slip of paper resting on the toilet tank. A Home Depot invoice with a photocopy of a returned check attached. He studied the name and address on the check copy while he dried his hands.

"Well, pleased to meet you, Mr. Hollister," he chuckled, crumpling the papers and burying them beneath a pile of used tissues in the trash next to the toilet.

He froze, listening intently. Moving silently out of the bathroom, he slunk to the living room and stood still, listening. A light breeze blew in through the open windows, stirring the mesh curtains. He turned to the front door and dropped into a crouch. For a moment, the only sound came from the radio in the kitchen. Suddenly, the door crashed open, swinging from broken hinges. Tear gas canisters crashed through the window screens, filling the room with a haze of chemical smoke. Black-clad SWAT team members burst through the door frame in respirators and full body armor.

Beams of light crisscrossed the room from flashlights clipped under the barrels of their assault rifles.

Griffon whirled as the back door shattered and more SWAT officers swarmed in. Smoke rapidly filled the room.

"On the ground! On the ground *now*! Hands behind your head. Do it *now*!"

Griffin let his face go slack and complied. One officer stood over him, the barrel of his M4 aimed at his head while another landed with one knee on his back and cuffed his wrists behind his back.

"We clear?" said the man aiming at Griffon.

"We're clear," said a voice from the kitchen. "Sir, you'd better come back here."

The team leader stepped away from Griffon's prone form, another officer immediately stepping into his place. He crossed to the kitchen where a group of officers were huddled, staring at something partially hidden by the door.

The walls and counters were bathed in streaks of blood and gore, running in the crazy patterns of a psychotic abstract painter. Behind the island counter, a pair of nylon-clad legs protruded, ending in bloody knobs where they had been torn off at the knees. White bone and cartilage glistened under the florescent lights.

To call the room an abattoir would be an insult to abattoirs. Bits of flesh and muscle lay scattered across the floor and a slimy blood trail led around the corner to the side.

"Where's the rest of her?"

"Something over here," said another officer in a shaky voice, pointing at the sink.

The team leader walked to the sink, sidestepping the pools of blood on the floor. He peered inside, ignoring the gagging sounds from the other men in the room. In the sink lay an eyeball, a gangly network of nerves still attached. The blue iris stared back at him, the whites shot through with a spiderwebbing of thin red lines.

"What the fuck did he do to her? Check the knives, power tools. Everything. Anything. There's still a lot of body missing."

"Sir," said an officer standing at the edge of the blood trail at the opposite end of the kitchen. He vomited into an empty evidence bag and stepped back. The team leader edged the crime scene and peered around the corner.

"Aw, Jesus…"

. . .

Hollister pulled up across the street at the address Griffon had given them and killed the engine. He leaned across the cab and stared out the passenger window. The retaining wall lay exactly where Griffon said it would be, but it fronted the drive through ATM lane of a Union Bank. Security cameras covered the entire area, including the corner spot where the diamonds were hidden.

Hollister cursed, then laughed in delirium and exhaustion. When his laughter subsided, just before the point of devolving into tears and screams, he pursed his lips and stared at the wall. He took a deep breath and started the truck, driving back to the safe house.

. . .

Goodwin and Chiha were heading back to the FBI office when Goodwin's cell rang.

"Goodwin."

"They found her." Rollie Barnett, sounding excited.

"Great work, Rollie. Let's not move too fast and spook her. What's the address?"

"She's way beyond spooking, Dave. "

"What?"

"House in Long Beach. Neighbors called in about loud music and screams. Got license plates on Lewis's car. Got a description of the man, too. It was Griffon. SWAT rolled in a few minutes ago. She's dead, Dave."

"*Shit!* Griffon?"

"In custody. But Dave, this was way out of his zone. She was … she was in pieces when they found her."

Goodwin wrenched the steering wheel and screeched a U-turn in heavy traffic, causing a collision behind him as he sped down the street, not caring.

"Give me the address. Tell them not to touch anything. And no one talks to Griffon until I get there!"

"Right. But SWAT's been running this one. You know how that goes."

*"Fuck!"* He cut the call and focused on driving.

. . .

The car slid to a sideways stop in front of a police barricade and Goodwin jumped out. The house and yard were crawling with local law enforcement. Pelican area lights staged around the perimeter illuminated the yard, now cordoned off with police tape. Patrol officers pushed back a group of neighbors trying to get a view of what was happening.

Goodwin motioned for Chiha to follow and badged the cop at the barricade.

"He's with me," he pointed to Chiha.

The cop moved the sawhorse to create an opening and the two men slipped through. A news helicopter circled overhead as they walked up the driveway to the shattered front door. On the lawn a detective screamed into a hand mike for someone to get the fucking chopper out of the area. A group of SWAT officers stood in the drive next to what he assumed was Lewis's Porsche, their faces pale as they smoked cigarettes and spat on the ground. A forensic team brought a gurney up to the front door, covered with empty body-storage bags.

"Multiple bodies?" Goodwin asked.

"Multiple body pieces. This is one for the books," said a Japanese lab tech.

"What happened to her?"

The tech pushed his eyeglasses farther up his nose.

"You'll have to ask Hannibal Lecter in there."

A commotion in the side yard grabbed Goodwin's attention. The SWAT team emerged on the grass, surrounding Griffon as they hustled him towards an unmarked police car parked at the curb. Two detectives followed.

"Just a goddamn minute!" Goodwin shouted as he ran to them, holding his ID in front of him. "Special Agent Goodwin. He's an escaped prisoner. He's mine. I have jurisdiction here."

One of the detectives turned to meet him.

"Hold on. We can sort everything out down at the station. We'll handle the transport. No need for a pissing contest here."

"I've been running ragged after this guy for almost a month. I'm not taking any chances with this. I'll transport."

The SWAT team continued to walk Griffon to the car. The other detective opened the back door and shoved him inside.

"Hey!" Goodwin shouted. "Hey, get him out of there and put him in my car!"

"No. That's not gonna happen. He's in our custody until we get everything sorted out at the station."

Goodwin reigned in his frayed emotions.

"Look," he said, "he's an escaped felon who killed a guard and four inmates up at Redwood. It's federal."

"Yeah," the detective sneered, "well he also tore a woman to pieces back there," he jerked his thumb to the house. "And we can't find a murder weapon, so he must have used his hands and teeth on

159

her. That makes him *ours* until we get to the station and sort this shit out. You got a problem with that, you take it up with the watch commander."

The detective headed to the car before Goodwin could answer. He climbed behind the wheel and hit the siren, inching forward as officers moved the sawhorses blocking the street. As the car passed, Griffon looked out the window and stared at Chiha. Their eyes met, and they shared a look of recognition. Griffon nodded his head slowly, grinning as the car drove off and headed downtown.

. . .

Two blocks from the safe house, Hollister pulled to a stop when he saw the flashing lights and crowd of police and onlookers. *Shit*, he thought, *mother fucking shit*. He slammed his hands on the steering wheel. Panic rushed through his nervous system, flooding him with adrenaline. He turned the truck around and drove off into the night.

# CHAPTER 2

Griffon sat in a metal chair behind a table. The cinderblock walls of the interrogation room reflected the glaring lights off their freshly-painted white surface.  Across the table sat a fat detective in rumpled clothes, flipping through a file of crime scene photos. His younger partner stood near the door, his heavily-muscled arms folded across his broad chest, staring at Griffon with barely concealed rage. The seated detective continued to inspect the photos in silence while Griffon sat passively, his wrists cuffed to the chair, head tilted to one side.

"You know," the detective sighed, spreading the photos on the desk one by one as he spoke, "this is why the prison system just don't work.  What happened, Jake?  You get fucked in the ass one time too many up at Redwood?  That why you snapped? Go in as some pissant cartel errand boy and come out as Jack the fuckin' Ripper?"

Griffon looked at him, perfectly calm.

"Ripping up four scumbag inmates, and that shitstain lawyer ain't gonna keep you from riding the big needle this time, Jake. You killed a prison guard this time. That's a one-way ticket to death row. Only thing I don't get is why you just stabbed the guard. Your buddies pull you off before you could go to town on him? That why you ate them out in the woods? 'Hard Time Jake,' huh?  Maybe we should change that to 'Wolfman Jake.' That's what the boys at the crime scene started calling you."

Griffon twitched a micro-smile.

"That's funny to you? Let me dumb this down for you then. You got one card left to play. You give up the diamonds and maybe we can keep you alive. I just want you to know this ain't my idea. Up to me and we wouldn't even have this conversation." His eyes flicked to the mirror on the side wall.

Behind the one-way glass, Goodwin stood, flanked by the D.A. and the Homicide Captain. All six eyes were riveted on Griffon on the other side of the glass.

"I still say I don't like floating life without patrol on this one. If anyone deserved lethal injection, it's that man," said the captain, pointing at Griffon through the glass.

"Politics, Bill, just politics. Besides, one trial for the state crimes, another for the federal. He might be dumb enough to fall for it if he talks before he asks for council."

"One thing he isn't is dumb," Goodwin added.

Both men turned to look at him.

"Why haven't you pressed him on the escape?" Goodwin asked.

"We'll get to it. Not relevant at the moment. We've got murder one with torture and cannibalism right here in our backyard. Everything else is backstory."

Goodwin turned to the DA.

"I need to talk to him."

"Once he's transferred, you can talk to him all you like."

"How long?"

"Once the jurisdictional bullshit gets sorted out. There's you, there's us, there's the prison guard's union screaming up in NoCal for the trial to go down up there."

"I need to question him now, not after the red tape cutting."

The captain turned to face him.

"Then you should have done a better job at getting him before he got hungry here. Right now he's in our custody, and we'll deal with him as we see fit."

"You guys don't know what's going on here. You don't know him."

"Then why don't you tell me? In fact, where's your boss? Why are you the only Fed dealing with this?"

Goodwin turned crimson, stammering for a reply, then left the room without comment, slamming the door behind him.

. . .

The sun was low in the morning sky, but the street was quiet in the pre-rush hours. Goodwin wearily exited the station and descended the steps to the parking lot. Lack of sleep piled on top of the fatigue and his slide into an adrenaline crash left him nearly broken as he shambled to his car. He climbed into the driver's seat beside Chiha, who appeared to be asleep.

"What is happening?" Chiha asked, his eyes still closed, startling Goodwin.

"Jesus, don't you ever sleep?"

"What is happening?"

Goodwin sighed, "They won't let me near him. They have themselves a celebrity killer, and they've all gone into 'fuck the feds' mode."

"Tonight, he will complete the change."

"Then we'd better hope like hell he's transferred out of here before then. Meantime, I'm going home to sleep for a few hours. I'm dead on my feet as it is. Then I'm going to start with the owner of that house. Trust me. Griffon's not going anywhere for now."

Chiha gave him a look of such pain and desperation that he flinched.

"Look, there's nothing we can do now. After a little sleep, I'll be sharper and can think this through."

He started the car and turned onto the street, Chiha staring out the passenger window as the city came alive in the growing morning.

. . .

Hollister sat in his air-conditioned truck, listening to the radio as the engine idled in the credit union parking lot. Sweat poured down his face despite the icy air pumping from the vents.

*... say Griffon was apprehended at a house in Long Beach last night. Griffon, who escaped last month from Redwood State Penitentiary along with two other prisoners, is the prime suspect in their brutal*

*murders, along with corrections officer Joseph Paulson. At the scene in Long Beach, police discovered the body of Rachel Lewis, 37, whom Griffon had retained as his attorney two weeks prior to his escape. Police would not comment on whether or not they believe Griffon is responsible for her murder, or if Lewis was suspected of any involvement in his escape. A press conference is scheduled later this morning at the Police Administration Building. In other news, local fishermen are protesting ...*

"Shit! Shit, shit, *shit*."

Hollister snapped off the radio and laid his head against the headrest. He closed his eyes against the tears leaking through his lids. If the cops had Griffon, then he'd no doubt spill everything about Lewis. About *him*. He wiped his face with a handkerchief and headed towards the credit union, his face set with grim determination at what he knew he had to do. Rachel was gone. Nothing would change that. All he had left were Cindy and Tanner. His stride increased as he pushed out all other thoughts and focused on the plan.

# CHAPTER 3

By late afternoon, the shadows of the October day had lengthened as the sun arced towards the Pacific. Goodwin lifted the crime scene tape stretched across the front yard and headed to the front door, Chiha following behind.

"Here," he said, handing him a gold FBI Investigator's badge on a lanyard. "Put this on. It won't do much good if they ask for ID, but it should do for a few minutes."

Inside the house, two forensics people were still at work. A crazed spiderweb of red strings radiated from several central points, marking the trajectory of blood splatter in the kitchen and side room. Goodwin slung the lanyard for his ID over his neck as one of the techs, a thirtyish blonde woman with a pageboy haircut, looked up from the spot on the floor she had been searching.

"Don't get up. Bad one, huh?"

"I got here at three this morning, so I didn't see the body … what was left of it anyway, but yeah. This one makes the Night Stalker look like a librarian."

"Murder weapon?"

"Not so far. They figure it was some kind of heavy blade, but everything in the house is clean. From the splatter, we know that most of the wounds were pre-mortem, but … you familiar with this guy?"

"Yeah, a bit."

"Lucky you. They said that some of the wounds looked like

166

post-mortem bite marks. There's still some pieces of her missing, but we're still looking. Is this really a cannibal killing?" Her eyes showed a little too much interest in gory case aspects, but how any lab geeks could do this job and not be drawn to the dark side was beyond Goodwin's comprehension.

"Bathroom?"

"If you need to puke, use one of those," she said, pointing to a stack of ziplock bags on the counter. "We haven't swabbed the toilet and sink in there yet."

"No. Just snooping."

"Back there and turn left. First door on the right.

"Thanks."

He turned to Chiha, who stood in the corner, breathing slowly through his nostrils.

"Why don't you wait for me in the car," he whispered as he walked past.

He walked down the hall and put on a pair of plastic gloves before pushing the door open. The room looked clean, but the stench of blood hung heavily in the air. The sink and toilet looked somewhat clean. When SWAT broke in, they found Griffon with a clean face and wet hair, so he had to wash up somewhere. He scanned the shelves and the space between the sink counter and baseboard. Nothing. In the waste basket he saw several wadded up tissues covering something. He reached in and withdrew a crumpled invoice with a photocopied check stapled to it. He read the name and address printed on the check, then folded the paper and slipped it into his hip pocket.

He left the bathroom and hurried out to the car. Chiha rested against the hood, drawing stares from the two patrolmen outside as he sniffed the air occasionally.

"Hey, said one of the patrolmen, starting towards him. "Hey, hang on a sec."

"In the car. Now." Goodwin said, and Chiha moved like a man in his twenties as he opened the door and dropped onto the seat.

"*Hey*! I saw your ID last night, but no way Tonto there's an agent. *Hey*!"

Goodwin was behind the wheel and pulling away from the curb before the cop could get halfway across the yard. He slapped the bubble light on the car top and lit it up.

"That should cover us for a while, but someone's going to call my office soon about you."

"There is another scent. There were too many people here last night, but now I am sure. The other man who met Griffon on the street. He has been here. His scent is all around."

"Want to pay him a visit?"

"You know who he is?"

"Not personally, but I know where he lives."

He pulled the invoice from his hip pocket and handed it to Chiha. As Chiha read the address, Goodwin's cell rang.

"Goodwin."

"It's Barnett. Your boy's being transferred. They're moving him to Metro until jurisdiction gets settled. LA's going for a full court press on this one. You want to talk to him, you'd better get down there, 'cause it's already a media circus."

"*Shit*. Got it." He clicked off the cell.

"He's being transferred to a holding facility downtown in a few hours."

"We must get to him."

"What am I supposed to do if I can get in to see him?"

"Nothing. You did not create this. You must bring me to him. I will end what I have begun."

"Bring him to you?" He laughed. "He's being transported in a corrections van under heavy guard to the biggest jail around. What, do I just walk up and say, 'Hey, hate to bother you guys, but this prisoner is really a werewolf, see? I just need to bring him to another werewolf friend of mine who will take care of everything. Easy-peasy, right guys?' Shit, they'll have me on a 5150 before you can say full moon."

"Just get me there. And drive faster. There is not much time."

Goodwin shook his head and stomped on the accelerator, speeding towards the setting sun.

. . .

The drive to the police station was excruciatingly slow, end of work traffic congealing the lanes like a blocked artery. Even with the light flashing, they only made it to the jail just before sunset. The evening sky was shading to indigo as they inched onto First Street.

A crowd of reporters huddled on the sidewalk outside. Cameras clicked and lights shone brightly on a group of uniformed officers concentrated at the front doors and a smaller group blocking a drive on the side. Goodwin turned on the radio:

*... has been the subject of a manhunt spanning three states since his daring escape from Redwood State Penitentiary last month. Now a suspect in the brutal slaying of the local attorney he previously retained, Griffon will be transferred to Metro jail where he will await trial on six counts of murder and mayhem. Details of the killing of attorney Rachel Lewis have been sketchy, but sources inside the department have confirmed that rumors of dismemberment and cannibalism are in fact true. Griffon has not been cooperative with police so far, so we may need to wait for the trial before gaining insight into his descent into extreme psychopathic violence...*

"Fuck me, we're too late," Goodwin said, slamming the steering wheel with his fist. Chiha watched with him as a police transport van pulled out of the garage and turned onto the street.

The crowd of reporters turned to give chase, shouting questions at the moving van. The steady clicking of cameras escalated into a steady mechanical rhythm and news vans pulled out to follow the van as it turned out of sight.

"Now what?" asked Goodwin.

"You go and find this other man." He looked to the East,

170

where a faint orange film of light hinted at the rising moon. "Soon I will be able to follow Griffon better than you. You have done all you can. The responsibility is now mine."

He moved to open the door handle. Goodwin put a hand on his arm, then quickly withdrew it as he felt the writhing of muscles beneath his jacket. It was like touching a sack of rattlesnakes. Chiha looked at him with large, swimming eyes.

"I must go. I must kill him. The other man is for you. He is of your world. Griffon no longer is."

Goodwin swallowed the blockage that had risen in his throat. Chiha stood up from the passenger seat and closed the door. Goodwin pulled away from the curb, relieved to be away from the only hope he had of seeing Griffon brought down. As he drove, he looked in the rearview mirror, but Chiha had already disappeared in the growing twilight.

## CHAPTER 4

Hollister pulled into his driveway and killed the engine. He had put off the final showdown with Cindy as long as he dared. He began strong, walking into the credit union and emptying the joint accounts he had with Cindy, leaving a hundred dollars each in checking and savings.

"Are you sure you want to do this, sir?" asked the teller. If any outstanding checks or charges come in, you could run a negative balance."

"*Yes!*" he nearly shouted, then calmed himself. "I'm sorry, I mean yes. We're going to Las Vegas, see. A second honeymoon. I know it sounds crazy, but I just have a feeling that luck's with us on this trip."

The teller smiled nervously.

"Besides, I have payment for a big job coming in by the time we get back, so the account will be fine."

*Robbing Peter to pay Paul*, she thought.

"Would you like me to issue you a bank check? It would be safer than traveling with cash, and I'm sure your hotel would be happy to cash it for you in their casino."

"No, no," he said, easing into the lie. "I like the cash. Makes us feel like big shots. Like in the James Bond movies. All part of the romance, you get it?"

She had seen gambling addicts come through her line before,

but could never get used to their desperation, their lies.

"I guess," she said, demonstrably uncomfortable.

She counted out the cash and placed it in several envelopes for him. He left before she could ask any further questions. He repeated the same withdrawal from his business account at a different bank across town. The sum total was just short of twenty-five thousand dollars. He thought about his 401k, but knew it would take at the very least a few days to get access to the cash, and he was out of time.

His confidence wavered as he left the last bank, and he stopped into a bar to steady his nerves. He ordered a Jim Beam and slammed it down, then signaled for another. The booze hit him fast, quickly gaining control over his exhausted brain and turing his thoughts cowardly. Rachel was gone. Gone in the worst way. As much as he had come to hate her over the past two days, he still yearned for his pipe dream of sunny beaches and tropical drinks. A life of sex and booze and an endless supply of cash tucked away in a very secretive bank.

*I can do this*, he thought as he ordered a third drink. Flush the dreams; go back to Cindy and Tanner. Even if she balked and went to the cops, he could still get away with some seed money. But he dreamed a new dream. Cindy would be pissed, but given the option of facing the cartel's wrath, she would come with him. They could move to the Midwest, start over. Raise Tanner in a small town and work as a laborer or mechanic. New names, new identities. A chance to reset the clock and start over.

He lost track of the number of drinks he ordered and drifted into alcoholic time, where the booze slowed the clock and two hours became five minutes. When he looked out the windows, he saw that night was coming on fast. *Shit. Shit, you're gonna give up the sauce, too.* He paid cash for the drinks and rushed to his truck.

And now he sat, looking at his home. The neighborhood was quiet and no cars were in front of the house. He removed the envelopes of cash from the glove box and ran up the walkway, ignoring the frantic attention of his golden retriever that rushed to greet him as he burst through the front door.

. . .

The moon had begun to crest the hills to the East as the police van wound its way through evening traffic on its way to Metro. In the back, prisoners sat in two rows facing each, swaying back and forth as the van cruised along. Their wrists and ankles were manacled and linked through a connecting chain as they sat in silence.

The prisoner across from Griffon was nearly as large as Bastien, head shaved, neck tattoos rising from a denim shirt buttoned to the top. He stared at Griffon. Griffon stared back. The contest held for several moments.

"Jake Griffon. 'Hard Time' Jake, huh? You don't look like no hard timer to me."

Griffon held the stare, the corners of his mouth turning

174

upwards in the tiniest of grins.

"Think you're king shit of turd pond? Cops, Feds all looking for yo' ass an' shit?   You headin' back now though, boy. You nothin' but a little bitch on the inside.   You got somethin' to say, boy, or you just gonna sit there an' smirk?"

Griffon broke into a wider grin that showed his teeth. He rested his head on the van wall and began to shake.   Thin capillaries stood out in the whites of his eyes, starting near the bottom.   They slowly connected and began filling his eyeballs, clouding them a bright red.   The red slowly shifted to orange.   Griffon blinked.

"Show time," he said in a guttural voice.

In the front of the van, the driver gripped the wheel as all hell broke loose in the back.   Shouts and curses turned to screams and growls.

The driver took his foot off the gas.   "What the fuck's going on back there?"

The escort turned to look through the mesh screen into the back, shining his flashlight through the grate. All he could see were a tangle of bodies thrashing in a writhing mass, the loud growling sound raising the hair on his arms.

"*Hey!* Sit the fuck back down, Goddammit!"

A spray of hot blood splashed across his face through the screen.   Momentarily blinded, he heard hideous ripping sounds and several heavy thumps as the screams died one by one.

"What the fuck's happening, Tolland?" shouted the driver. "Talk to me!"

A massive impact punched the metal mesh outward from the back, hitting the driver in the head. The van careened in traffic, swinging from lane to lane as the tires squealed.

"Oh fuck, oh fuck, oh fuck!" Tolland repeated, wiping blood from his eyes.

Another blow punched the twisted grate fully out, driving through the back of the driver's head and into his skull. The van shot across an overpass above a flood channel. The driver's hands dropped from the wheel, and the van crashed through a guard rail and plummeted over the edge to crash onto the concrete floor of the channel, its front end accordioning on impact. In front, the two officers flew about the cab like rag dolls as the van settled back and rocked to a stop. Smoke poured from the crushed engine. On the overpass, traffic slammed to a stop. Reporters tailing the prison transport leapt from the news vans and began filming into the darkness below, unable to see much in the gloom.

The passenger door creaked open, and Tolland crawled out onto the channel floor, dazed and bleeding. The driver lay against the side door, his head halfway out the shattered window. Tolland saw brains and shattered bits of skull leaking out the gap in the back of his head. He limped to the back of the van, his gun drawn.

"Unit fourteen, unit fourteen," he said into his shoulder mike, "Emergency. Transport vehicle crashed. Officer down. 11-99, I repeat officer down."

He staggered on his feet, hand falling from the mike. The rear door was still intact. No sound came from what lay behind.

Then he saw the blood running out from the bottom and over the bumper in a thick waterfall. His jaw dropped and a loud thud ripped the door from its hinges, knocking him to the ground as it fell on him. He struggled to move the door off him, but lay helplessly pinned as he saw two small orange lights glowing in the back of the van. An impossible shape emerged, bloody saliva dripping from its huge teeth. Tolland felt his sphincter release as the shape rose on its hind legs and sprang on top of the door pinning him. The weight crushed the air from his lungs as he stared into a horror from his childhood nightmares.

It was covered in thick black fur matted with fresh blood and bits of flesh. Two long ears rose from a skull that ended in an elongated snout filled with long wolf teeth. It's back was humped and thickly knotted with muscle and sinew, impossibly long legs and arms extending out, ending in long claws with curved dagger tips. It lowered its head to Holland's, covering him in a carrion stench that made him retch. Before he started screaming, Holland was sure that it curled its lips around its teeth in a rictus grin.

It leapt to the side and tore the door off of him, flinging it far into the flood channel. Holland watched in horror as it raised a hind foot and placed it on his stomach, pressing down with crushing force. The creature raised its head and loosed a deafening howl into the night, arms raised in triumph. The reporters on the overpass fell back from the sound.

Then it tilted its head to look down at Holland, the smile returning to its muzzle. It pressed down harder and twisted its hind foot on Tolland's stomach, sharp claws cutting through his uniform and flesh. Holland screamed as his intestines spilled from the wound, squelching between the beast's claws as it ground them to a pulpy mess. Holland spasmed and felt a coldness wash over him. Then the beast dropped to all fours and buried its maw in the wound, snapping up bits of intestine and chunks of flesh. It reached the backbone and snapped it between bloody jaws, crunching the bone as it chewed.

Holland felt nothing below the waist as it ate away at his midsection, his twitches slowing as he lost consciousness, and then his only movements were those caused by the relentless tearing and rending as the beast continued to feed. It finally raised its head to the crowd gathered on the overpass and snarled before turning and looking up the flood channel to the hills in the background.

From their vantage point, the crowd on the overpass caught a glimpse of a dark shape running on all fours across the dark flood channel and up the hill on the other side, vanishing over the crest into the darkness beyond.

. . .

Cindy stood from the couch when her husband burst in, but he brushed past her, dropping the envelopes of cash on the coffee table before he hustled up the stairs to their bedroom.

"Greg, where the hell have you been? Where are you going?"

She charged up the stairs after him, finding him in the bedroom, rummaging through dresser drawers and tossing clothes on

178

the bed. He pulled a passport out of the nightstand drawer and added it to the pile.

"What are you doing? Where are you going? Talk to me, Greg! What's going on?"

Hollister turned and took her arms in his hands.

"Not me. Us. We're getting out of here now. No time to explain, but some very bad people may be on their way, and we have to get out. *Now*."

"Greg. Greg, just stop. Stop it. Sit down and we can talk. "Please Greg, you're scaring me."

Hollister began adding her clothes to the pile on the bed. He kicked through the junk at the bottom of the closet.

"Where are the goddamned suitcases?"

"*Greg!*" she shouted, snapping him out of his search. "Greg, what kind of trouble are you in? What happened?"

He turned to her.

"I … I can't. We just have to go now."

She moved in closer.

"Jesus, have you been drinking?"

He bolted past her and thundered down the stairs. She began to follow and nearly slammed into their son, who emerged from his bedroom, rubbing his eyes.

"Mommy, what's going on?"

Cindy softened her voice against the runaway panic.

"Honey, go back to bed. Go on, it's okay. I'll come in and tuck you back in in a second. I promise."

She steered him back into his room and closed the door, then sped down the stairs. Outside, the dog was barking madly, shut out when the door slammed after Hollister's hysterical entry. She found her husband pulling a shoebox down from the top shelf of a closet. He poured bullets from the box into his jacket pocket.

"I told you I never wanted the gun in the house!"

"These are bullets. The gun's in a lockbox in the truck. Just grab the stuff upstairs and something for Tanner. Throw it all in trash bags. No time for the suitcases."

The raw panic in his voice stilled her tongue.

"Come on, move!" he yelled as he reached for the front door and threw it open.

He took a step onto the front landing, then froze, his hands out in front of him. He took a step back into the house. Behind him, Cindy screamed.

# CHAPTER 5

Goodwin pulled up in his car just as Hollister ran in the front door. He listened through the open car windows as raised voices competed with the barking dog for volume control in the quiet neighborhood. He thought about calling it in, but then reconsidered. He needed to talk to Hollister alone first, see what he knew about Griffon. He was running so far off the procedural grid that he needed a telescope just to see it.

Movement in the upstairs window drew his attention. Hollister was tossing clothing on the bed while a frantic woman pleaded with him. The whole scene screamed fast getaway. Time to move.

He exited his car and walked up the sidewalk to the house, drawing his gun as the barking dog turned to him. The barking increased in pitch, but the dog looked friendly, wagging its tail and lifting its front paws off the grass. Goodwin reached down to scratch its head, then straightened and proceeded to the front door. As he stood in front of the door, it flew open as Hollister took a step across the threshold and froze when he saw the gun. He raised his hands and stepped backward into the house, moving slowly. In the front room, the woman screamed.

"Who ... who are you? Don't shoot, we have a child. Please," she cried, shaking at the sight of the gun.

Goodwin pulled out his ID while keeping the gun trained on Hollister.

"I'm not planning on shooting anyone. My name is David Goodwin. I'm a special agent with the FBI, and I'm here to arrest your husband, not to hurt anyone, so lets all just take a slow breath and calm down here, okay? No one wants this to go south, right Greg?"

Hollister stood frozen in place, but gave a slight nod of his head. Cindy backed up until her heels bumped the first step of the staircase, and she sat down, her eyes wide with shock and fear.

"Arrest him for what? Greg, what's he talking about? What have you done?"

"Aiding and abetting a fugitive for starters," Goodwin said. "Conspiracy, accessory to first degree murder ... you've been a busy boy, Greg."

"I don't know where he is."

Cindy started to cry.

"I do. He's most likely on his way here. We need to get you out now, both of you."

"Why? Who are you talking about? Who's coming? This is crazy, my husband wouldn't kill anyone. Greg, tell him!" Her words defended her husband, but the tone was less certain.

"A very dangerous man. He's probably already broken out of custody. Trust me ... you don't want to meet this guy."

Cindy started to cry again, dropping her head to her hands. Hollister looked from his wife to the gun in Goodwin's hand.

"You said you had a child, Mrs. Hollister," Goodwin said in as calm a voice as he could muster.

"Yes," she wailed. "He's upstairs. Jesus Christ, he's just a little boy."

"I need you to go get him. Don't scare him. Just tell him we're going for a ride and do it quickly."

"Why do you need us? I have no idea what *he's* been doing." She pointed an accusing finger at her husband.

"Move! *Now!*"

Cindy reacted as if slapped and scrambled up the stairs, leaving Hollister and Goodwin alone in the room.

"I was just trying to take care of them. No one was supposed to get hurt."

Outside, the dog had moved to the back yard. The barking continued, then abruptly stopped.

"Yeah, well life is full of surprises, Greg. How was no one supposed to get hurt in a prison break? Getting in bed with a guy like Griffon was supposed to be a quick one-night stand? At least seven people are dead. God knows how many more before the nightmare you helped unleash ends."

Cindy came back down the stairs, carrying a sleepy boy in her arms. He was crying softly, face buried in her shoulder.

"Okay, let's go. You first."

He reached around Hollister and opened the front door, pushing him through from behind. A flurry of movement flashed in front of Hollister and he staggered back a step, turning as he slumped to the floor. A line of deep gashes stretched across his abdomen, entrails spilling out onto the floor. As Cindy and the boy screamed, Goodwin kicked the door shut and fired two shots through it. A rumbling growl ascended into a shriek of animal pain on the other side.

"It's the monster! It's the monster!" Tanner screamed.

"Oh my God, Oh my God! *Greg!* Oh my God call an ambulance! Oh my God!"

Goodwin backed them to the stairs, blocking their view of Hollister's body.

"Is there a phone upstairs?"

Cindy nodded, deep in shock.

"Take the boy and call 911. Now! Go!"

Cindy backed up the stairs, carrying the hysterical boy. Her eyes locked on her dying husband as she retreated.

Goodwin turned and bent to Hollister. Dark blood leaked from his mouth as he lay dying.

"Take care of them. Please," he whispered as a bubble of bloody saliva formed on his lips.

From upstairs, Cindy shouted, "The line's dead!"

"Use your cell!" Goodwin shouted.

"It's in my purse down there."

"Fuck!" he whispered. "Lock all the windows and get away from them. All the downstairs doors locked?"

"Yes… I think so." Her crying drifted down the stairs like a mournful ghost.

"Good," said Goodwin looking down at Hollister. "Stay up there. No matter what you hear, don't come down here. Just stay up there with the boy."

Hollister clutched his ruined stomach, staring at him through bloody eyes. Goodwin knew what he had to do, but balked at the thought. Steeling himself, he pointed the gun at Hollister's head and pulled the trigger twice. Screams erupted upstairs.

He reached into his jacket for his cell and pulled it out, gliding to the sliding door in back. He checked the door and drew the blinds, then headed for the kitchen. He began punching 911 when the kitchen window exploded inward as something large and furry crashed through, knocking into him. The phone flew from his hand and skidded across the kitchen floor, sliding into the space between the refrigerator and the counter. He spun and fired blindly at the shape. Bullets thwacked into the ruined body of the golden retriever.

"You're a smart motherfucker," he said as he moved to kill the kitchen light. Outside the broken window, he could see the thing that used to be Griffon staring at him a few feet away. Gore smeared its animal face as it ran a long tongue across its teeth, licking off the blood. A bullet wound marked one hairy shoulder. Goodwin fired his gun, but the beast moved in a flash, gone like a puff of smoke in a high wind.

The screams upstairs evolved into muttered sobs as Goodwin hugged the wall back to the living room. A thud that shook the house battered the heavy front door, which held despite the cracks in the frame. Goodwin dropped to a crouch and emptied his gun at the door, the acrid smell of gunsmoke filling the room. Animal shrieks of pain drowned out the screams from upstairs. Then silence from

185

outside. Goodwin slammed another magazine into the Glock and racked the slide.

He swung the gun from the door to the windows, listening intently. He rose to a crouch and inched his back up against an interior wall. Upstairs, he heard the boy crying as his mother tried to soothe him. The night breeze blew through the broken window in the kitchen, carrying a musky scent along with it. He turned back to the door and tried to reason a way out.

Behind him, the dog door flap on the side door into the kitchen lifted silently as a long arm drenched in bloody fur reached up and slowly turned the deadbolt. The arms withdrew and the knob turned silently.

Goodwin advanced down the hall, sweeping the room with the gun. He turned at the kitchen and once again looked to the battered front door. He smelled an overwhelming carrion odor behind him and spun, firing blindly. The impact of the beast when it sprang drove him across the room and white-hot pain flared in his shoulder as it bit him, teeth sinking deep into his muscle and resting on bone. The gun dropped to the floor and discharged, the bullet whizzing past his ankle. He felt himself fly across the room as a monstrously strong arm flung him backhanded, crashing into the door and nearly knocking it from its hinges.

As the beast curled on its hind legs to spring, he grabbed a lamp from the table in the doorway and swung it in an arc, driving it into its head. He heard the eye pop as the bulb shattered and the sizzle and stink of burning flesh filled the room. The beast shuddered as the current passed through it, blue sparks leaping from the burning fur on its face. It howled in agonized rage, and threw Goodwin across the room. He somersaulted through the air and crashed through the banister at the foot of the stairs, landing in a bloody heap.

The beast, one side of its head smoking and charred to the skin, raised up on its hind legs and slowly advanced, murderous rage in its orange eyes. Goodwin shot a glance to the gun on the floor and prepared to dive, but the sound of crying from upstairs caused the beast to look up. It slowly lowered its head back to Goodwin and grinned, its rage sliding into pure malevolence.

"If you have to kill me, then get it over with motherfucker," Goodwin panted. "Just leave them alone and get the fuck out while you can."

The beast turned its head back to the top of the stairs and advanced. Goodwin dove for the gun as the front door shattered open and another beast entered, ducking its head as it crossed the threshold. Taller than the first, its sinewy body was covered in grey fur. Gold eyes radiated light from their sockets. It let out a deafening howl as it stood, clawed hands clenched into fists at its side. The Griffon-beast returned a gargling howl as blood flowed over its lower jaw. The two creatures circled each other in the room, snarling and snapping.

Goodwin could feel the growing energy in the room as both creatures tensed their muscles, building strength that erupted as they collided. The battle exploded so quickly that all Goodwin caught was a flurry of movement, claws and teeth snapping and tearing, blood spraying the room in great geysers. He slipped in the blood and skidded on his back to the gun. He rolled onto his stomach, gun arm extended and prepared to fire.

The grey beast lay on its back, huge gashes covering its body. The black beast, equally wounded, painfully lowered its muzzle and gripped the other's throat in its jaws.

"Here, doggy doggy."

The beast snapped its head to him as Goodwin fired four shots that blew its brains out the back of its head, spraying the wall with pinkish-white splatter. It toppled backward to the floor and lay still.

Goodwin staggered over to the grey beast. To Chiha. To his friend. Chiha bled profusely from too many cuts and gashes to count. Too fucking many.

"Fuck. Fuck, this doesn't look good."

He bent to one knee and looked in his filmy eyes. Chiha nodded his wolf's head. Griffon pointed to the bite on his own shoulder.

"This doesn't look good, either."

Chiha looked at the wound and closed his eyes as he let out a long and mournful howl that echoed throughout the house. He opened his eyes, no longer yellow, and gave Goodwin a look of guilty pain.

"Yeah, I know." Goodwin winced as he moved his shoulder. "Bad night for all of us. I know what I have to do."

Chiha's wolf-face softened, and his breathing grew more shallow. Goodwin reached a trembling hand to the bloodied face and rested it on his brow. He drew his hand over the eyes, closing them as Chiha let out a final breath and lay still.

"Hey! Is everything over down there?" Cindy's voice drifted down the stairs.

"Everything's fine. Stay up there. The police will be here soon," he shouted.

"I have to see Greg. Is he going to be okay?" her voice now from the top of the stairs.

Goodwin rose to his feet with a groan. The room swam around him for a second, then leveled out. He moved to block her descent. She stopped flat when she saw him.

"You ... you're bleeding!"

"I'll be fine. But you need to stay up here. You can't help your husband, but your son needs you. I'm sorry, but that's the best I can do."

He leaned on the railing and tried to hide his buckling knees.

Cindy burst into fresh tears and ran back to the bedroom. Goodwin watched until she entered and shut the door. Leaning heavily on the railing, he returned to the carnage downstairs. The bodies of Griffon and Chiha had shifted back to human form, making their wounds all the more grisly. He looked down at Chiha and gave a sad smile.

"You lost the battle, but we won the war. I hope things go easier wherever you are now."

He walked to the sliding doors and ripped down the curtain, tearing the rod off the wall. His strength was already returning. God knew what else would accompany it. He draped the curtain over Hollister's body. Bloody flowers bloomed on the white fabric, but it was better than seeing his wounds naked and raw.

Walking to the kitchen, he opened cupboards until he found bottles of vodka and gin. Grabbing a box of kitchen matches from the refrigerator top, he walked back to the living room, drenching the bodies with alcohol. He shouted upstairs as he poured.

"Mrs. Hollister, I need you to bring your son downstairs, and come to me. Keep the boy's head covered and keep looking at me."

He grabbed her purse from the couch and stuffed the blood-splattered envelopes of cash from the coffee table inside.

Moments later, she appeared at the foot of the stairs, her hand on the back of Tanner's head.

"That's good," he said. "Just keep looking at me."

She was crying, but did as he asked, holding fast to his eyes like a lifeline.

"You have your car keys?"

"In my purse," she nodded.

"Good." He ushered them into the shattered doorway and turned to strike a match and toss it into the pool of alcohol. It caught in a whoosh that followed the flowing channels on the floor and reached the bodies.

"What are you doing? Jesus Christ are you crazy?"

"That may be up for debate, but I need you to listen to me."

He handed her the purse, wads of cash sticking out the top. He grabbed her by the arm and spoke straight and hard.

"Take this. Take your son. Get out of here and start a new life. Forget what you've seen and forget what you've heard. Forget me. No one would believe you anyway."

"But you … you can't do this. You're the FBI."

"Yeah, well I'm changing careers."

Tanner squirmed his head around from under his mother's hand.

"I told you there were monsters," he said.

"Kid, I wish I could say you were wrong." He looked at Cindy. "Now *go*, go on!"

He shoved her out the door and watched as she hurried to her car and placed the boy in the back seat. She had just turned the corner onto the cross street when the first sirens came howling through the night air, floating along below the huge hunter's moon that moved inexorably towards the Pacific.

# EPILOGUE:
## NORTHERN CALIFORNIA, 2018

The man packed the old canvas rucksack for a hike. Along the walls of the cabin, a variety of modern additions – canned goods, a propane stove, books, a radio –mingled with the old wooden carvings and tapestries. His hair longer and a full beard covering most of his face, he exited the cabin and set off down the trail to the East.

He walked through the forest, surefooted and alive to every sound, every movement. He passed groves of trees and continued along the high banks of a fast-moving river, following it upstream as it passed between towering rocks lining the water.

Later that evening, smoke rose from a campfire in a clearing on the crest of a ridge. The first stars appeared in the twilight sky. Goodwin sat naked before the fire, looking out over the lower hills towards Redwood State Penitentiary, waiting for the moon to rise.

. . . . . . . . . . . . . . . . . . . . . . . . . . . . . . . . . . .

Connal Bain spends his free time causing general mischief and bloodying the decks of his blog thebigadios.com, where he reviews crime and horror fiction and film. His hobbies include drinking far too much coffee and dreaming up talk-show banter that he'll probably never get to use. *Blood Moon Fever* is his first novel. He can be reached by fans of all things weird and scary at ConnalBain@gmail.com.

Made in the USA
Las Vegas, NV
16 August 2023